ANOTHER CHANCE TO GET IT RIGHT

A New Year's Eve Anthology

Edited by Nicole Frail

www.andyoupress.com

Trigger Warnings: *Child Abandonment,* Infant Death,* Divorce,° Death of a Parent^*

Arrangement copyright © 2024 by Nicole Frail

"All Year With Anthony" copyright © 2024 by Katie Fitzgerald; "Righting My World"^ copyright © 2024 by Shirley Hay; "Fia"* copyright © 2024 by Sharon Thatcher; "Dancing Queen" copyright © 2024 by Jessica Daniliuk; "I'll Be Home for New Year's?" copyright © 2024 by Krista Renee; "What One Would Do for a Rose" © 2024 by H. Buckley; "New Year's Baby" copyright © 2024 by Anna Picari; "Seeking Sanctuary"° copyright © 2024 by Desi Stowe; "Polka Dots" copyright © 2024 by Mitchell S. Elrick

This book is a work of fiction. Any references to historical events, real people, or real locales are used fictitiously. Other names, characters, places, and incidents are products of the author's imagination, and any resemblance to actual events or locales or persons, living or dead, is entirely coincidental.

All rights reserved. No part of this publication may be reproduced, distributed, or transmitted in any form or by any means, including photocopying, recording, or other electronic or mechanical methods, without the prior written permission of the publisher, except in the case of brief quotations embodied in critical reviews and certain other noncommercial uses permitted by copyright law.

For permission requests, publicity requests, or other inquiries, write to nicolefrailbooks@gmail.com.

To order in bulk or to sell this book in your retail brick-and-mortar or online store, contact nicolefrailbooks@gmail.com.

Cover design and interior illustrations by Kerri Odell
Edited and typeset by Nicole Frail/Nicole Frail Edits, LLC.

First publication: November 2024

www.nicolefrailbooks.com | @nicolefrailbooks | www.andyoupress.com | @andyoupress

Print ISBN: 978-1-965852-06-4
Also available as an ebook.

Contents

Introduction   1
by Nicole Frail

"All Year With Anthony"   3
by Katie Fitzgerald

Gwen, an event planner, organizes a New Year's Eve party, but she's not happy with how the evening unfolds. She is comforted by Anthony, the sweet sous chef with whom she has shared many happy memories this past year.

"Righting My World"   17
by Shirley Hay

It's been ten years since Claire's life changed forever on New Year's Eve. At a party, with memories threatening to break her, she must decide what kind of love she's worthy of receiving.

"Fia"   33
by Sharon Thatcher

A recluse living in a remote area of the Scottish Highlands is confronted with a peculiar conundrum on New Year's Eve: an abandoned baby in the forest. Her traumatic past comes back to haunt her as she tries to save the child who is on the brink of death.

"Dancing Queen"   **51**
by Jessica Daniliuk

Quinn goes to her favorite club on New Year's Eve expecting it to be like every other weekend. Everything changes when she meets a guy named Peter.

"I'll Be Home for New Year's?"   **63**
by Krista Renee

Ella and Lulu are looking forward to their first New Year's Eve together as a married couple; however, as an OBGYN, Ella knows she'll be lucky if she gets out of L&D before the clock strikes midnight. Lulu holds out hope that Ella will join her and that she'll bring news they've both been waiting for with her.

"What One Would Do for a Rose"   **79**
by H. Buckley

George Callander returns home, dreaming of a picture-perfect reunion. But after years of drifting in and out, always in pursuit of fame, he finds his family on the verge of collapse. By midnight, George must make a life-changing decision.

"New Year's Baby" — 93
by Anna Picardi

Avery Fellows has always felt cheated by her New Year's Eve birthday, overshadowed by holiday celebrations and everyone else's plans. As she grows up, she struggles to find joy in a day that never seems to be just hers—until a chance meeting and new love change everything.

"Seeking Sanctuary" — 109
by Desi Stowe

Priscilla is beyond tired of people telling her what to do. In desperate need of a new beginning, she's seeking sanctuary and hoping that, on New Year's Eve, she might find it.

"Polka Dots" — 135
by Mitchell S. Elrick

Two roommates-slash-best friends set out on an adventure to help one get a date with the girl of his dreams on New Year's Eve.

Contributors' Library — 165

About the Editor — 166

Introduction
Nicole Frail

Thank you for selecting *Another Chance to Get It Right: A New Year's Eve Anthology*! This is the second title to launch from a new (super-small) independent press, and we all thank you for the support you've already shown us with your interest in not only a new title from a new house, but a collection of stories that includes some brand-new voices, too!

When most think of New Year's Eve, they envision celebrations: champagne, loud music, the ball drop and countdown, fireworks and kisses. They make resolutions, they plan ahead, they want to be better and do better. The New Year brings with it a fresh start, a new beginning. A second (or third, or fourth, etc.) chance to try again. For many, New Year's Eve symbolizes hope.

But for others, it can be a reminder of the boxes that went unchecked, the goals that were not achieved, and the people they left behind. A new start can be intimidating. Sometimes it's easier to stay put and hide behind what you already know well.

The characters in the stories presented on these pages experience a wide range of emotions as the end of the year draws near for them—emotions that accurately represent the ups and downs that come with starting over, starting something new.

You'll cheer for those who are lucky enough to get that longed-for first kiss at midnight. You'll grieve with those who take a moment to cherish the memories of friends and family who are no longer with them. You'll sit and sympathize with others who are faced with impossible decisions and deadlines as the minutes tick away. And you'll celebrate those who realize that they don't need the New Year to do better and be better but that the nudge it provides isn't always a bad thing.

We hope you enjoy this mix of short stories and that you have a Happy New Year!

All Year With Anthony

Katie Fitzgerald

"FIVE ... FOUR ... THREE ... TWO ... ONE ... Happy New Year!" The crowd in the hotel ballroom clinked their glasses and sipped champagne, but Gwen was out the kitchen door like a shot, heading into the frigid night air without looking back.

The important moments of the party were over, and she'd done her best, but she was sure there was no way it had been enough to impress her boss, the perfect and unrelenting Corinne. Corinne had made her instructions clear: "Wow me tonight, or I'm letting you go." Wow her. Ha. New year, same old impossible expectations.

The balloon drop Gwen had planned for midnight had been canceled due to a delayed balloon delivery, the desserts had been half the size of what she had expected, and only half of the catering staff had gotten the memo about the dress code. The list of flaws in this celebration could probably fill a whole page in the planner in which Gwen had diligently laid out the perfect night. She figured it didn't matter if she watched the whole thing crash and burn or not; the disaster she'd put into motion would happen with or without her at this point.

It was cold, though. She'd been hot inside with all the dancing bodies in their fancy gowns and tuxedos, but out here in the parking lot, the plain white blouse and slacks that made her look professional yet unassuming were far too thin against the winter chill. She hugged herself, rubbing her hands along her upper arms as puffs of her breath sailed toward the stars.

"Gwen?" The sound of her name in a tentative male voice caught her attention, and she glanced toward the kitchen exit.

"Anthony," she breathed as she realized it was the sweet sous chef from the catering company who had been trying to help her all night. Even in this miserable mood, the sight of him lifted her spirits just a touch. "What are you doing out here?"

Notes of "Auld Lang Syne" slipped through the crack in the door where he had left it propped open.

"You disappeared," he said gently. "I was worried." He was wearing a white double-breasted chef's jacket, which he began to unbutton. Though it left him in short sleeves, he draped it over Gwen's shoulders. "Happy new year," he said.

Gwen breathed in the smell of onion and basil. That smell always made her think of Anthony.

"I don't know how happy it is," she said with a sigh. "Corinne is probably counting up my mistakes as we speak. This has been a train wreck."

Anthony shook his head. "That's not what I saw in there."

"You were busy," Gwen protested. "Trust me. Corinne is going to have my head on one of those shiny silver plates with lids."

"That's called a cloche," Anthony corrected, smiling fondly. "But that's not going to happen."

"You're always so optimistic," Gwen chided. This was probably her tenth time working an event with Anthony, but only the third one where she had been in charge. The first and second experiences hadn't gone so well, and Corinne had an immovable "three strikes and you're out" policy. Gwen was sure Anthony was only being nice, as he always was to everyone. "But Corinne will tell it like it is, so you may as well, too."

"Corinne is a jerk," Anthony spat bluntly. "She thinks a perfect party is one without a crisis. But I've been in this business almost eight years, and I know that a perfect party is one where every crisis is managed." He put a hand on Gwen's shoulder. "You were a rock star tonight. Everyone in there had an awesome time, and that's down to you."

Gwen knew her body temperature couldn't actually have risen ten degrees in an instant, but it really felt that way when Anthony made contact. He was warmth personified, this man. She would miss seeing him all the time when she inevitably got fired.

"How do you do that?" she asked, pulling his chef jacket tighter around her shoulders.

"Do what? Compliment you?" He flashed a grin. "They just roll off the tongue. It's easy to tell someone her good qualities when she has so many."

"Not that," Gwen said, her face definitely blazing with heat now. He really was the nicest guy. "Just . . . how do you stay so positive?"

Anthony seemed to think for a moment, then he shrugged. "The alternative is depressing, I guess. I don't know. I prefer the bright side. It's not like you can go wrong with happy thoughts."

"Auld Lang Syne" faded out, and Gwen heard people clapping.

That didn't sound terrible.

As if reading her mind, Anthony said, "See? They loved it. That applause could just as easily be for you. Because you made the magic happen."

"But it could have been so much more magical!" Gwen complained. "You should see what I planned!"

Anthony pointed at her. "That right there," he said. "That's how I stay optimistic. I focus on what is, not what might have been. Only you know how different the party looked in your imagination. Nobody else knows that. To us, it just looks like a brilliant event planner threw an amazing party."

Gwen replayed Anthony's words in her mind for a moment, trying to reframe the night from his perspective. Quite a few guests had complimented the unique flavors of the appetizers Gwen had selected. She certainly had no reason to believe they would go out of their way to say nice things if they didn't mean them. The sound system had also worked perfectly because, unlike the two previous times she had been in charge, Gwen had remembered to test everything twice at the beginning of the night. It seemed like a small thing, but only because everything had gone smoothly. It would have been a huge ordeal if the speakers had failed or the microphones had died suddenly.

She shrugged. "I don't know. With Corinne in my head, it's hard to know if anything I do is good enough." Anthony had a point, though. She was always so worried about getting even one tiny thing wrong that she had stopped noticing any time anything went well.

"Get her out of your head then," Anthony said.

More sounds from inside crept through the doorway: first the muffled sounds of the DJ speaking, and then the opening notes of a slow dance ballad.

Gwen recognized it as an old, nostalgic favorite. "Oh, I love this song."

"In that case, I know how we get her out of your head." Anthony said. Before Gwen could admit that she had no idea what he was talking about, she found him in her personal space. She was surprised but pleased when he circled her waist with his arm, resting his other hand on her shoulder. "Dance with me?"

Gwen knew she should probably worry about getting caught goofing off, or possibly getting frostbite, but somehow, in Anthony's sure, firm hold, she found that all her concerns about work felt less pressing. Relaxing her shoulders and releasing a slow breath, she stepped in closer to Anthony and wrapped her arms around his neck.

"Better, right?" he said gently.

"So much better," she agreed. *Corinne who?*

For a few moments, they were silent. Gwen didn't know what Anthony was thinking about, but she was taking inventory of all the moments she had shared with him this past year. There were more than she realized.

When they had first met by the fountain outside of the country club in April, she had noticed the deep brown of his eyes, and the floppy curl that hung over his forehead. She turned to look now, and she found it was still there, just tamed tonight with gel to keep it neat. It was adorable, she realized. She had always thought so.

In July, the poolside fiftieth reunion she'd helped host for a nearby high school's alumni had required lots of heavy lifting, as furniture was rearranged, coolers were hauled, and grills were positioned. When Gwen's arms nearly gave out beneath a stack of lounge chairs, Anthony appeared from seemingly nowhere, rushing to her side to balance the pile before Gwen could collapse beneath it. His muscles had taken on the weight like it was nothing.

Remembering how kind that he'd been at the summer event, when his real assignment had been to prepare gourmet hamburger toppings, she now pressed her fingers into those appealing biceps. "You're so strong."

Anthony laughed. "You think so? Watch this." Carefully, with complete control, he supported Gwen's back with the palm of one hand and dipped her toward the asphalt.

"Wow," she said, truly impressed. It felt like her heart flipped over in her chest as he slowly pulled her upright again. "Strong and smooth," she teased.

"You know it." Anthony flashed a cheesy smile that told Gwen his cockiness was a joke.

As he drew her in close once again, her memories resumed, coming quicker.

In August, Anthony had accidentally walked in on Corinne chewing Gwen out over a spill that had resulted in a slip-and-fall injury for one of the guests at a fundraiser. Without a word, he had gone back to the kitchen and made her an ice cream sundae, which he delivered to her on the sly as soon as Corinne was out of sight. They ended up sharing the sundae, spoonful by spoonful, as Gwen vented her frustrations over the accident. He had listened, and asked questions, but he also seemed to know that she didn't want advice. She just didn't want to be alone in the aftermath of such a harsh dressing-down.

Oktoberfest had been the night Anthony brought the kitchen to a halt when he realized they were making the wrong appetizer, one with an allergen that certainly would have killed one of the guests of honor. The only reason he knew was that he had chatted with Gwen about the menu earlier in the evening. He always paid attention to her, always anticipated what she would need, and prevented trouble from finding her. How had she not realized before?

December had brought a flurry of holiday parties, the last of which was tonight's. She understood now that the late-night cups of cocoa they had shared after each Christmas gathering had probably not been coincidental occurrences. Anthony must have stayed late just to grab those last moments together. He must have wanted to stay with her.

The song Gwen loved came to an end, but as though the DJ knew the moment needed to linger, he immediately faded into another ballad, this one even slower.

"Anthony," Gwen said, her fingers gently smoothing his hair. "Are you even on the clock right now?"

Anthony's cheeks were already pretty red from being out in the cold, but his eyes had a caught look in them that told Gwen she had figured him out.

"I was sent home an hour ago," he admitted sheepishly. "I was on set-up, not clean-up."

"You stayed for me." Gwen spoke her realization aloud as it occurred to her.

"Is that a problem?" For the first time, she saw a tiny ripple in his steady optimism, but she quickly put his concerns to rest.

"Not in the least," she said. Pulling back, Gwen sought Anthony's eyes until she had steady eye contact. "I love spending time with you."

Anthony lifted a hand to her cheek, and though the music hadn't stopped, he no longer swayed to the beat. They both stood completely still, and then Gwen felt a giddy spiral of joy spin through her as Anthony leaned down and pressed his lips to hers.

Gwen had always romanticized midnight New Year's kisses,

but she'd never had the opportunity to experience one. This one was a bit past midnight, and she was only dressed in her work clothes, and it was extremely cold standing in the lot behind the venue, even with Anthony to keep her warm, but no kiss could have been more perfect.

"I really hope you didn't do that just to distract me," Gwen said, laughing nervously, finding that she felt punchy and her lips still tingled.

"Uh uh," Anthony said, seemingly lost for words as he cradled her head and brought her mouth to his once more. "I've wanted to do that all year."

"All ten minutes of this year?" Gwen teased, and he playfully shoved her shoulder.

"All of *last* year," Anthony said. "Is that clearer? Ever since you started working with Corinne."

"So you're telling me she's been good for something after all?"

"You know me and my silver linings," he quipped. "Some good comes out of everything."

Gwen gazed up at Anthony, noting that his curl was beginning to lose its shape. Soon it would hang down over his forehead again the way she liked. She wanted to be there to see that, but the sound of her name snapped her back to the reality of her situation.

"Gwendolyn," came Corinne's stern voice inside the kitchen. Gwen was being summoned.

Even the most amazing kiss in the world couldn't change the fact that she was still at work, still probably about to be ripped to shreds and then fired by her tyrant of a boss. She swallowed hard, feeling her mouth go dry.

Eyes wide, she looked up at Anthony, but he gave her shoulder a reassuring squeeze. As she slowly removed his jacket and handed it back to him, Gwen felt a renewed sense of confidence. So what if Corinne, who barely knew her, and saw her, at best, as the help thought she was a failure? She didn't have to judge herself by impossible standards. Anthony believed in her, and, if she removed fear of Corinne from the equation, she also believed in herself. In fact, why wait to be fired?

"Don't leave, okay?" she told Anthony. "I still want to be able to see you after I quit my job."

Anthony's eyes widened. Then he gave her a warm, genuine smile. "Good for you. Let me go grab my stuff. Meet me back out here, and we can go grab a cup of cocoa at the diner to celebrate."

Gwen started to move toward the kitchen door, then paused in her tracks. "How about a kiss for luck?" she asked, giving Anthony a mischievous little grin.

Anthony leaned down and gave her a peck on the lips, followed by a longer, slower kiss that curled her toes. "You don't need it," he said. "But any excuse to kiss you works for me."

Smoothing her shirt and quickly neatening her hair with her fingertips, Gwen squared her shoulders. However Corinne reacted when Gwen resigned, she knew she could face it now. Whatever vitriol Corinne had to spew would be counteracted by sweet words from Anthony, not just tonight, but all year long.

About the Author

Katie Fitzgerald is a homeschooling mom, trained children's librarian, and short story and flash fiction writer. Her short contemporary romances appear online at Spark Flash Fiction and Micromance Magazine and in several anthologies, including *Wither and Bloom* (Twenty Hills Publishing, February 2023), *A Winter Promise* (Dragon Soul Press, December 2023), and *12 Days of Book-Club-Mas Volume VII* (Once Upon a Book Club Box, Fall 2024). She is also the author of *Library Lovebirds*, an ebook collection of bookish romances (September 2024) and a novel in flash, *The Bennetts Bloom* (January 2025). Katie lives in the Maryland suburbs of Washington, D.C., with her librarian husband, four daughters, and one son.

You can find Katie on:
Instagram @katiefitzstories

And visit her website at https://bio.site/katiefitzgerald

RIGHTING MY WORLD

Righting My World
Shirley Hay

I KNOW THE PRECISE MOMENT my world shifted on its axis. In fact, it was the very same moment I'm in right now. "Auld Lang Syne" was playing through a tinny loudspeaker, lights flashed off a cheap disco ball, glassy-eyed people swayed and kissed and laughed too loud. I stood so confidently then, ten years ago, my life mapped out as precisely as my fourth-grade lesson plans.

At twenty-four, I'd had the job and the car and the apartment and the guy. Soon it would be a house and kids and Tuesday-night soccer. I remember glancing at my ring as I leaned in to kiss Aaron, strobe lights dancing across his stubbly face. He smelled like sandalwood.

My phone was already ringing. I just hadn't heard it yet.

I look up and see Mia coming toward me. She has Ian by the hand and is dragging him through the crowd. They're both clinking champagne glasses with people as they push through a throng of backless dresses and sweaty armpits, their cheeks flush with alcohol and marital bliss. Mia catches my eye and smiles. I can see she wants to get back to me, make sure I'm still okay. She only left my side to give Ian the obligatory midnight kiss, and only after I threatened to drag her over to him myself. But now she's back and, in spite of myself, I exhale.

Mia and Henry were the first friends I made when I moved from Edmonton to Winnipeg for school back in 1998. Henry sat on one side of me in Intro Psych, and Mia on the other. I must have looked like a lost puppy that needed rescuing or something. Or maybe they could just tell the difference between the locals and the transplants, since they were new to the city, too.

They both grew up in Weyburn, Saskatchewan, and had known each other forever. According to Mia, she'd met Henry in-utero as he graced the world with his presence. Mia's mother, a local midwife and eight months pregnant with her at the time, was the one on-call when Henry's mother went into labor two weeks early and the regular midwife was in Mexico. *I still remember the screams when his mother pushed out that giant head*, Mia had said with a wink.

They told me all of this within the first five minutes of meeting them, shooting finger guns at each other with little clicking sounds.

I could have told them I was an only child, or that my mother had raised me on her own. I could have told them that my father was listed as a missing person from the time I was four until six days before my tenth birthday when his remains were found in an abandoned farm shed. I could have told them his case was still unsolved. But none of that was as interesting or fun as their story, so I'd just smiled and nodded awkwardly at the blank notebook in front of me.

The next class, they sat in the exact same spots and told me a new story about Weyburn.

It took me a couple of weeks to realize that Mia and Henry weren't a couple. I started to piece it together when they'd bring up past boyfriends and girlfriends as casually as if they were talking about a plate of fries. I expected some uncertainty, that underlying tension couples have in these circumstances, even the most secure couples, but it wasn't there. Finally, one day I just asked them directly. Mia had stared at me like horns had suddenly sprouted from my head, and then they'd both burst out laughing. They must have laughed for at least five minutes—that wheezing, no-noise, bent-over kind of laughter. Coke definitely came out of Henry's nose. Turned out it was more of a brother-sister kind of relationship.

For a while it was just the three of us, which was a lot easier for me when I realized I wasn't third-wheeling. Soon, Logan and Annaleise (who *were* a couple) became affixed to our little triangle and we shifted into a pentagon. We all hung out a lot that first year, and the second. We left books and gym bags and coffee cups in each other's dorm rooms. We sat at the same table in the cafeteria so often we named it Fred. We proofread each other's essays and condemned politicians and quoted philosophers. We were cocky and brass and thought the world owed us something. We laughed over everything and cried over nothing.

Sometime during third year, Mia met Ian and things shifted again. We all still saw each other, spilling into each other's lives like waves lapping on the shore. Most days were still peppered with conversations and check-ins and favors. And we still debated politics around Fred, but sometimes the space got so crowded that someone had to move to a nearby table. At first, that was me. Then it was me and Henry.

Henry had always been able to make me laugh. He teased me and pranked me and goaded me into arguments about marshmallow roasting methods or the benefits of mechanical pencils. He'd pretended to detest elementary school teachers and Edmonton and Fords, just because I drove one. He'd known how far to go to get a laugh or a backhand or a smirk, and he'd known exactly where to stop. He was relentlessly obnoxious and implausibly kind.

Henry was the first person I'd told about the long years with my mother, and about my father's case. His was the literal shoulder I cried on when I told him that most kids at school knew me only as the girl with the murdered dad, or that I thought my mother was the strongest person on our unjust earth. He'd sat across from me and pressed his knee into mine when I told my story to Mia, and then to everyone else. He didn't make a big deal about anything; he was just there. Exactly where I needed him to be.

This was all before Aaron and his sandalwood smell.

Before Aaron's perfectly planned proposal at the lake at sunset, flawless and picture-worthy.

Before Mia married Ian, or Logan and Annaleise eloped to Lake Louise.

Before Henry became a travel blogger and globetrotted around the world for eight years.

And before 12:01 a.m. on New Year's Day 2005—the day I lost my mother and my carefully constructed future in one fell swoop. It would take a few days to realize it, but that was the moment my fate had been sealed.

"Claire!" Mia leans in now and hugs me tight. "Happy 2015!"

I hug her back and give her the same smile I use to greet my class of ten-year-olds every morning. I want her to think I'm having fun, but she sees right through me. We both know I'm no actress.

Mia wraps her arm around my waist. "I know, I know, you don't want to be here. But isn't this *a little* better than eating half a box of apple fritters and going to bed at ten o'clock?"

"Way better," I say, slipping in just enough sarcasm for only Mia to notice, then gulp the champaign Ian has thrust into my hand. I should have known that little admission last year would come back to bite me in the ass.

Mia has the memory of an elephant, and she's not above using embarrassing details to get me to do whatever she thinks is best. She's been trying to get me to one of these parties for almost a decade. She says it will break the association and help me move on. I glance at the disco ball and then hear the faint, phantom ring of my old flip phone.

She's definitely wrong.

I look over Mia's shoulder and see Annaleise and Logan coming in for a group hug. After they eloped, they moved to Vancouver for a few years, ready to hike and ski and party on Granville Street. But when Annaleise got pregnant with the twins three years ago, they packed up their thimble-sized Vancouver apartment and came home. Now they live in a cute three-bedroom in the south end. They have a dog and a fenced backyard and a play structure and a deck and a boy and a girl. Sometimes I imagine them as blue and pink pegs in a little car in *The Game of Life*. Roll. Move. *Twins!* Yippee!

I always smoke a little weed on my balcony after coming back from their place. *Parents can't do this*, I tell myself when I inhale. *I'm free as a bird.*

"Claire, we're so glad you came out this year," Logan says.

"Me too," I mumble into the mouth of my champagne glass,

then take a sip. I look over at Annaleise and notice a small stain on her off-white wrap. It looks like spaghetti sauce, or maybe chocolate. I realize I haven't asked about the kids yet.

"How are Charlie and Avery? I haven't seen them in weeks."

She leans in and grasps my forearm, a piece of blonde hair falling out of her updo. She laughs a tinkling sound that seems to have emerged with parenthood, and I wince. She was a hardass before. None of this cute-girl crap.

"Oh, *so* busy! It's just go, go, go—every minute of every day! You know how it is!"

I give her a tiny smile. She knows I don't. But maybe she can't think straight. I hear pregnancy kills brain cells, so twins must really do a number.

I look down and watch the few drops of my remaining champagne flicker and vibrate with the crowd of moving bodies. I try to think of something nice to say to Annaleise, but nothing comes to mind.

I wish I wasn't here. I'm kinder when I'm alone.

Mia is looking around the room again, as if she's expecting someone. I've asked her who she's looking for three times, but she always blows me off. A nightmarish fantasy suddenly emerges in my mind. Mia has invited Aaron and now he's there, pushing his way through the crowd, right to me. He tells me it was all a mistake. He tells me I should take him back. He tells me he wishes he'd stayed with me in Edmonton; that he should have never gotten in the car the morning of the funeral, taking off for home and leaving me alone. He tells me he wants it all back. The wedding and the house and the kids and the life we were building.

He tells me he's sorry.

That's when I punch him. I punch him so hard that his nose is crooked and bleeding. I punch him so hard that a loose tooth bulges against his swollen lip. I punch him again and again and again, until I can almost feel real pain in my right, clenched fist. Then I watch him stumble backward and fall into a table, a group of sparkly dresses parting like the Red Sea as he goes down.

"Claire? Earth to Claire!"

It's Logan again. He's asking me about my group of kids at school. Easy? Hard? Am I enjoying the break? Will I hate to go back?

I try to answer, but my voice catches in my throat. I can't do this anymore.

I excuse myself and move toward the washroom. It's full of people. My eyes are blurry, my head is spinning, and I bump into three different women before I find an unlocked stall. I collapse onto the toilet and feel the tears push past my eyelashes. One small sob escapes, and I cough, trying to mask the sound. I unroll a long strip of toilet paper and hold it loosely in my cupped hands, each fold and edge and pillowed dimple twisting with my memories.

I close my eyes, and I can suddenly see the little flip phone in my clutch purse from ten years ago. It rang eight times before I'd heard it that night. It was my Uncle Walt. For a long time, he hadn't said anything. I'd wanted to hang up, but I waited. When he finally spoke, he'd told me that my mother had been killed by a nineteen-year-old kid who had pre-gamed with some vodka shots before driving himself and his friends to a house party. Somehow, the kid had bypassed every checkpoint. My mother was walking the dog when he came skidding off the street and pinned her between the front bumper and the lamppost. The dog was okay. The kids had some scratches. There was blunt-force trauma to my mother's head. No one thought she'd suffered for long.

I'd hung up the phone and told Aaron that my mother was dead. He took a step back. He was trying to give me space, he'd explained later. I felt sick and ran for the door. After a few minutes, Aaron followed and found me throwing up in the bushes. I'd wiped my mouth and told him we had to go to Edmonton. He still stood so far away, but he told me he'd drive me there. It would be faster than finding a flight over the holidays. So, we'd taken a cab to our apartment and packed. Then Aaron had slept for six hours while I sat at the kitchen table, jabbing the tip of a paring knife into the soft wood over and over until it looked like a patch of pockmarked skin.

Sometimes, I still run my fingers over that spot of pitted wood.
When remembering hurts less than forgetting.
When touching the truth is all I can do.

I hadn't told anyone else about my mother until Aaron and I were halfway across the prairies, and only because Mia had called me in a panic, demanding to know why I'd left the party. I'd told her I was okay, and Aaron had offered to drive me home and I'd be back after the funeral and not to worry about me. I told her this was my cross to bear, and she had a wedding to plan. I told her to tell the others that I was fine.

Aaron hadn't spoken much on the drive or when we got to my Uncle Walt's house. But the next day, he'd found me in the kitchen and told me he hadn't thought everything through and wasn't sure what he was going to do about work. I asked him to call and explain and that I really needed him. He stood across from me, a deep frown creasing his brow. But then he sat down at Uncle Walt's desktop and emailed his boss.

The funeral was planned quickly. My mother had a lot of friends, but as far as family was concerned, it was only me and Uncle Walt. The decisions were made swiftly and, even at fifty-five, my mother had already purchased a plan through the funeral home. I told Aaron that we'd be able to go home soon and that I'd come back on my own during spring break to deal with the house. I didn't want him to miss too much work.

He'd gone for a walk.

I cried on the toilet.

The morning of the funeral, I woke up alone. I checked for Aaron's suitcase and saw that it was missing, too. I got into the shower and readied myself anyway, letting the hot water scald my raw skin until the heat turned tepid and unkind. His absence didn't surprise me. He'd always stood a quarter-turn from where I needed him. He always seemed ready to take a step backward.

In those moments, I wasn't even angry. I just knew it was over.

But as Aaron was driving away from me that day, Henry was flying to me.

I hadn't told anyone when or where the funeral was, but Henry had found out anyway. He'd sat at the back of the church as we sang my mother's favorite hymns, and he'd hovered at the edge of the reception hall as I greeted old neighbors and my mother's co-workers and the police detective who'd been our main contact about my father's case. Henry had smiled at me across the room and then hugged me in the reception line. I had no words for how grateful I had been that he'd found me.

Henry had been dating a girl back then. Savannah or Scarlette or something. She was mad at him for getting on a plane and coming to see me, but he'd said he didn't care. She was just throwing a post New Year's Eve party the following weekend and wanted him there. Apparently, she *needed* him there.

I'd sat across from Henry in my mother's kitchen as he told me this, two steaming cups of tea between us. I thought of Aaron's absent nod as I said the same thing to him only a few days earlier. What's a funeral if not a different kind of party? It was all so ironic and absurd, and I suddenly felt the truth of the past few years bury itself into my abdomen like a tapeworm, ready to feast.

I slipped off my ring and twirled it against my mother's wooden kitchen table. I mumbled a halfhearted apology for messing up Henry's relationship. He told me he couldn't care less about the opinion of some girl he barely knew. He told me Aaron wasn't worth the gum on the bottom of my shoe, and that I'd dodged a bullet by seeing his true colors this early. He pushed a dark brown curl from his eyes and told me I was his best friend, even better than Mia now that she spent all her time with "that Ian guy."

I'd chuckled and, for a split second, I found myself again.

Then Henry told me he loved me. I smiled and squeezed his hand.

I didn't know he'd meant *that* kind of love.

Mia told me later. Years later.

Someone is knocking on the stall door. I open my eyes. The wad of toilet paper is still in my hands, now crumpled and sweaty. I look at the gap between the bottom of the door and the sticky bathroom floor. Two pairs of heels are stationed in front of me.

"She's been in there a long time," a voice says. The words are slow and drawn out. I see one set of heels stumble a little.

"Maybe we should get someone," the other voice says.

"Who? A waitress?"

"I guess? Who else?"

More knocking. I take a deep breath and push myself to my feet, then unlock the door. The two women smile with relief and then ask if I'm okay. I nod and mumble a thank-you, then move past them to the sink. I wash my hands and run cold water over my wrists, trying to bring myself back to the present. I stop and find my green eyes in the mirror. Regret fills the space around me like an inflated balloon.

For months after my mother's death, I'd hibernated. Every ounce of energy I could find was poured into teaching my fourth graders. Henry had come by almost every evening, sometimes with Mia, sometimes with a group, and often alone. He'd taken me out to dinner and a movie the night Aaron came by to collect the rest of his things. He'd brought me apple fritters and dark roast coffee and movies on DVD. He'd sat next to me when I cried, and then he'd pranced around the living room in the frilly aprons I found at my mom's house, making me belly laugh. He'd listened when I told him how hatred filled my chest at night—for the kid who killed my mother, for the friends that didn't stop him, and for my mother for walking the dog so late at night on New Year's Eve. I told him that I didn't even miss Aaron, but I did miss the life we had planned together.

The day Henry left for his first trip to Australia, he'd asked me to keep his favorite coffee mug safe. When I'd seen him again, he asked me if I'd ever applied for a passport. And the next time he was planning a trip, he wanted me to take a leave of absence and go along.

I'd said no. When he asked why, I didn't have an answer.

He'd looked at me then, warmth and compassion and kindness filling his dark brown eyes. He told me I should find someone to love me exactly as I should be loved. He told me he couldn't wait to meet my future husband and the beautiful and brilliant children I was bound to create with whomever I chose. He told me I had been the perfect person to sit next to in Intro Psych. Then he'd kissed me on the cheek and walked out of my apartment.

That man would move mountains for you if you let him, Mia had said the next day.

That was six years ago.

We still text sometimes. I follow his travel accounts, share and like his posts. He sends me reels that make me laugh. Sometimes I respond, sometimes I just remember. I still have his coffee mug. It's on the top shelf, tucked way in the back. I know he wouldn't mind if I used it.

I hear Mia's voice outside the bathroom door. "Claire? Are you in here?"

"I'm here," I say, forcing the old smile back on my face.

"Well, thank God. I've been looking everywhere for you! Why do you disappear like that? Sheesh!"

I smile, a more genuine one this time. Thank God for people like Mia.

We link arms and head for the door. When we step into the crowd, she stops and scans faces again. Searching. I can see Ian and Logan and Annaleise, and I know she can, too, as she scans past them. But then her eyes focus, and I follow her gaze.

"Henry," she whispers. "Finally."

I almost don't recognize him. His hair is longer now, and he's bulked up from years of hiking mountains and learning to surf. But still, it's Henry.

Mia calls out and he turns to us. His eyes meet mine and his face softens. Mia hugs him and slaps him on the back and then tells him she'll get him a drink. He nods, but he doesn't stop looking at me.

Mia squeezes my hand as she leaves. She's always known. They've all known. It just took me a little longer.

It's time I right the world on its axis.

Henry pulls me close, and I let him hold me for a long time. Then he asks me if I'm still driving a Ford, and I jab him in the side and we both start to laugh.

This is exactly how I should be loved.

About the Author

Shirley Hay is an emerging author from the flatlands of the Canadian prairies. Her writing is informed by a background in psychology and family support, including neurodiverse children and those with mental health concerns. She writes about survival, strength, and slippery truths, always seeking to cage the shadows of a flickering world. Her writing has been published in *Suddenly and Without Warning*, *Creation Magazine: A Focus on Feminism*, featured on the podcast *Bookish Flights*, and in "50 Give or Take" from Vine Leaves Press. She is currently seeking a publication home for her debut novel, *Fault Lines*. Shirley lives in Winnipeg, Manitoba, with her family.

You can find Shirley on:
Instagram @shirleyhaywrites
Facebook @shirleyhaywrites

And visit her website at www.shirleyhaywrites.com

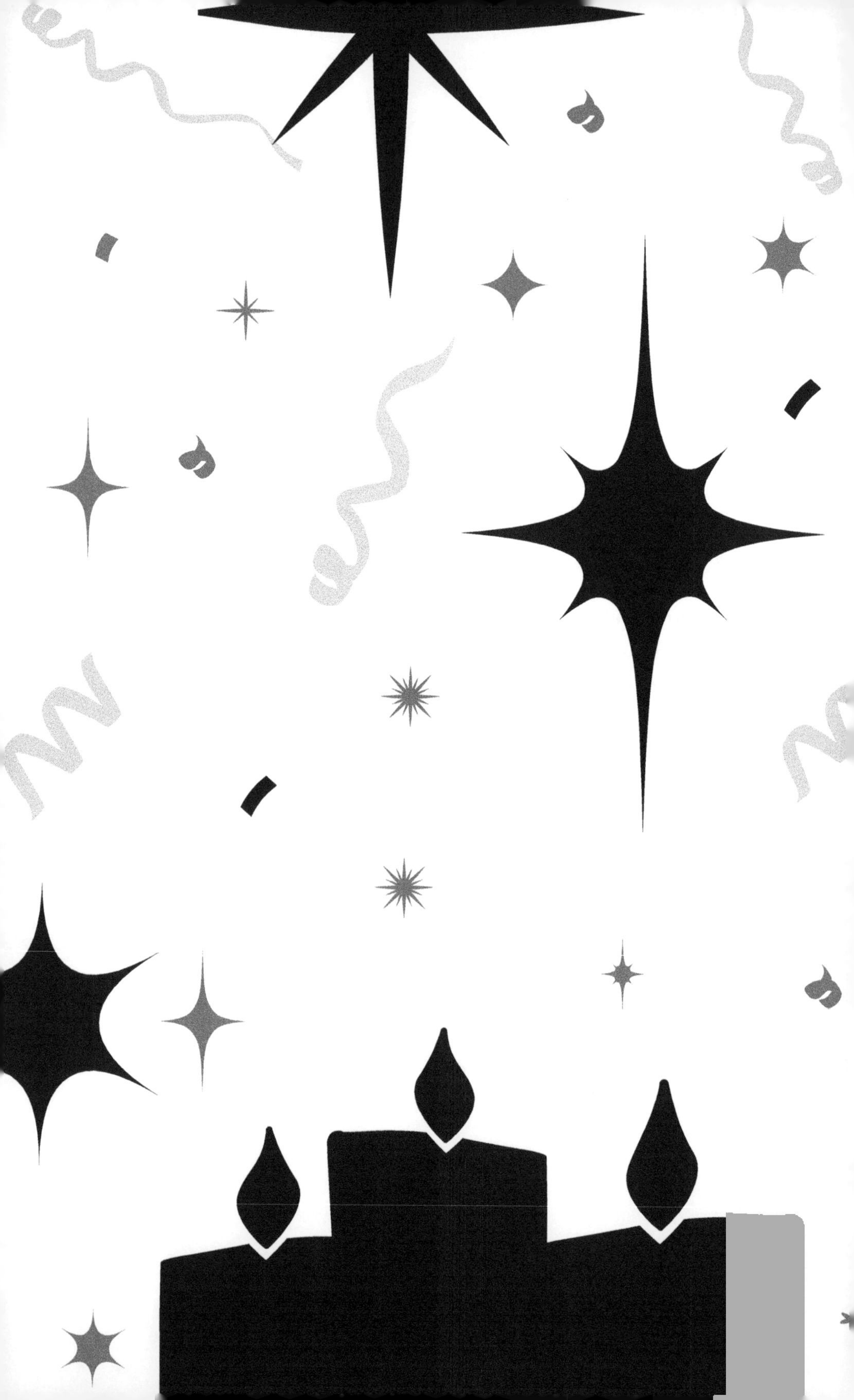

FIA

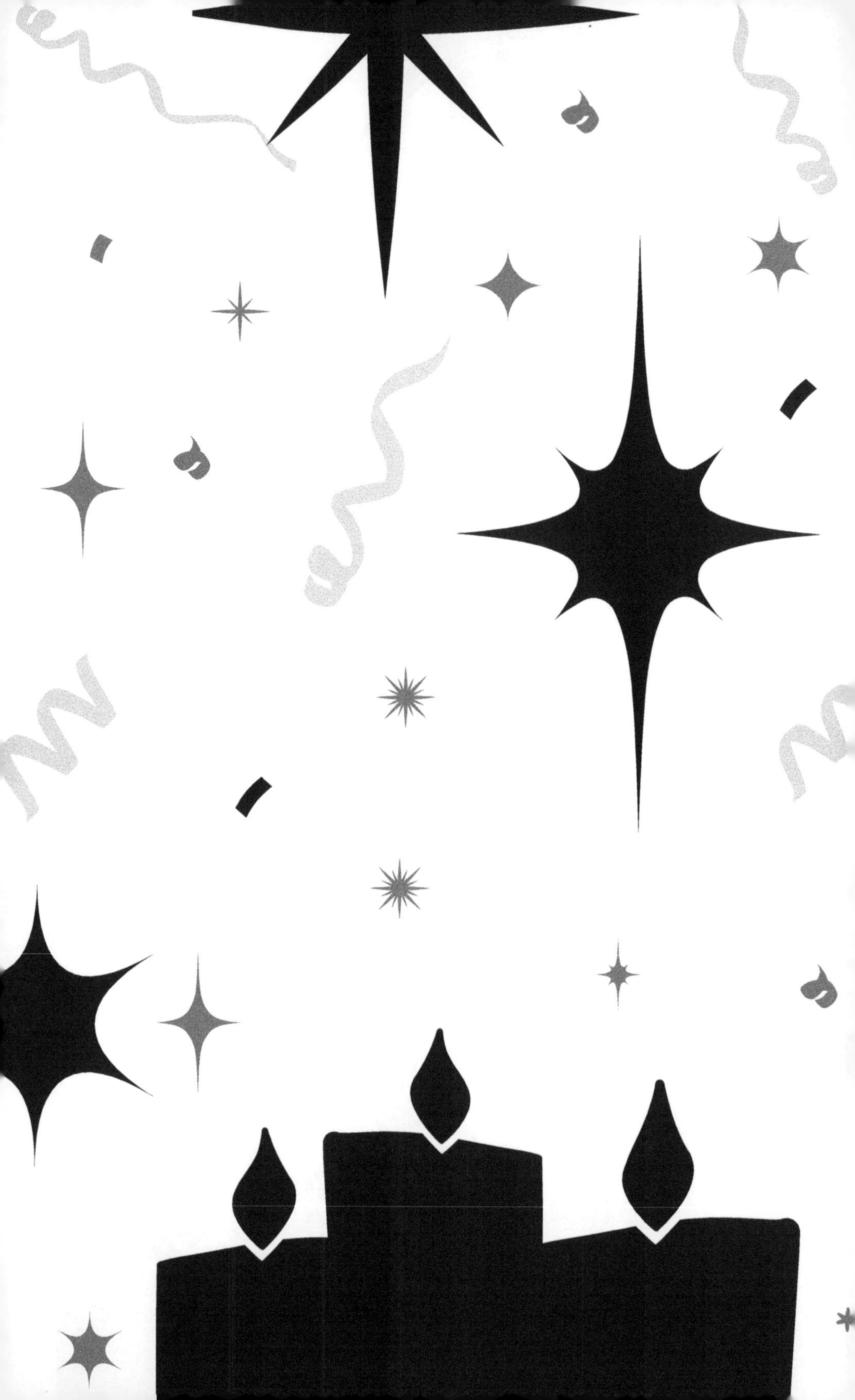

Fia

Sharon Thatcher

NESTLED AMONG THE MOSS-CLOAKED pines stood the lonely bothy. Its isolation was purposeful, its inhabitant reclusive. The icy waters of Loch Arkaig lay within a stone's throw, and the surrounding snowcapped mountains were visual reminders of the rugged and unforgivable landscape.

An aged woman shuffled through the forest, draped in shawls and donning a handknitted Fair Isle sweater. Her morning foraging had produced some mushrooms and wild garlic. As of late, her spectacles had become loose, often dropping down to the end of her small nose and crashing onto the stone floor of the bothy. She had little tools to tighten them but ironically needed the eyeglasses to fix them. There was no spare pair. As she crouched down to inspect the garlic, they once again slipped off her nose, and she heard the dreaded *crunch* as she shifted her feet to look for them.

"Oh, Fia!" she muttered, chiding herself.

She would have to go to Fort William, a forty-minute drive away. She rarely ventured out of her remote corner of the highlands and had no desire to. Her few semi-annual trips to the supermarket were done with careful planning and only out of dire necessity. In the wee hours, as soon as they opened, she would gather items, mostly dry goods, and use the self-checkout aisle. At such an hour, no one noticed her. With any luck, she could come and go without speaking to another soul.

To make these trips, she'd borrow a car from Angus, an acquaintance who lived five miles away in a nearby hamlet, using an old wagon to cart her precious items back to the bothy—oats, buckwheat, flour, sugar, long-life milk, eggs. She knew how to store these things properly so the damp wouldn't get in and she could survive for months on very little. She ate as she lived: quietly and simply.

A new pair of prescription glasses would be a different outing—one that would require social interaction and a couple of trips. Her career had been an undertaker in Glasgow, and then Shetland. Consoling mourners had never been part of her job description. Rather, she had always been more comfortable around the dead. They were her preferred company, but unfortunately for now, she had to remain in the land of the living until she could eventually join her quiet companions.

As she prepared for her journey, hoping Angus would be able to help with a vehicle, she suddenly remembered the date: Hogmanay. New Year's Eve. Maybe she should go another day, as he might soon be out with others, celebrating and making resolutions no one could possibly keep.

On her return to the bothy with the garlic and mushrooms from the morning's forage, she saw something through the green pines. An eerily silent bundle of brown blankets sat on a pile of stones. Although quiet, it appeared to be moving. Grateful her far-sightedness was stronger than her near-sightedness, she slowly approached. Though not naturally curious, she went to see what it was. No living soul had been seen in these parts for the better part of eight months. In the summer, few passed through on walking holidays and the like, but the temperatures were still in the single digits, dropping nearly to freezing at night.

Burrowed among the blankets, she could see the tiny features of an infant. She had no idea how old—perhaps only a few weeks. Reaching out to touch its forehead, the unfamiliar warmth of the child startled her. Glancing around, she looked for more movement. Apart from the gentle rustling of leaves in the perpetual wind that blew in these parts, there was nothing. She looked at the baby again.

This was simply none of her business.

Trudging on, she made her way toward the bothy to drop her findings. She prepared to go to Angus's and wondered if she should ring someone about the child. Pulling open old drawers and rifling through forgotten belongings, she found an old phone she saved for emergencies. Thus far, she had never used it. She switched it on and was not surprised to see there was no reception. She had been warned when she bought the bothy that it was unlikely mobile service would ever be accessible in these parts. Turning it off again, she tossed it back in the drawer.

As she prepared the old wagon that she always took to Angus's, an apparition of the child's face kept appearing before her. If she left it out there long enough, one of the foxes would no doubt appear. It seemed a grisly and unnecessary ending, really.

But what could she do?

She could see if it was still there.

Traipsing back, she found it was. She stood over it for a while, her aged mind working to resolve this completely alien conundrum. Hesitantly, she picked it up, its gentle weight unfamiliar and lack of response unsettling, and she returned to the bothy.

She noticed the eyes of the child were sunken, a sure sign of dehydration. That she knew. She opened a drawer, emptied the contents singlehandedly, and placed the child gently in the drawer. She lit a small fire, sat down in her chair and thought.

Nourishment was necessary of course, but what? She couldn't very well make up some porridge. This child needed to be fed from the breast, which was obviously out of the question. She wasn't sure if giving it water would help or not. Milk? She had very little left. How would she administer it? Could she warm some and pour it in its mouth?

For once, the quiet was deafening. Was it still alive?

She got up and felt it again. Still warm. A small rise and fall in its chest.

She would have to go for some supplies, and quickly. It was really the only option.

She set out, hoping it was not in vain. Pulling the wagon behind her, she made her peregrination slowly but steadily. Adding up the times in her head, she calculated that it would take the normal two hours or so to Angus's—that is, if he was about and his car was readily available—then forty minutes to Morrisons. There would be time spent shopping, another forty returning in the car, and a longer walk back to the bothy. Would the child even be alive? Was she better to try one of the small hamlets nearby?

She hesitated and peered down the path. Should she take the child with her and drop it off at the police station? How would she transport the child in the old wagon? The car? It's not like she had a car seat sitting around. What might Angus think? No, it required too much explaining and social interaction. At the very least, the child would be warm and protected inside the bothy.

Swirling thoughts consumed her as she walked, her tired legs already aching. Never having been a mother made this quandary baffling. She was completely at a loss for what to do.

In childhood, the nuns of Smyllum Park Orphanage withheld warmth and comfort, and Fia quickly learned to fend for herself, trusting no one. As soon as she'd left, she began her career at a funeral director's in Glasgow. The job suited her well. She'd come to enjoy her time with her silent companions, and she rarely socialized with her colleagues. Mr. Foster, the director of the funeral home, was reaching retirement and planned to have his son, who was also called Mr. Foster, take over the family business.

On his first day, Mr. Foster failed to mention to his son that no one really spoke to Fia, and in turn, she didn't really speak to anyone either. Thus, a young clean-shaven man with bright red hair bounded in gregariously. He interrupted her focus as she worked to embalm a body that had arrived that morning.

"Good morning!" he greeted. "I'm Rory Foster, Mr. Foster's son. As you know, I'm looking to take over the business eventually, so I am really looking forward to getting to know you and to learn everything there is to know."

Fia looked at him incredulously. He was certainly eager with his little rehearsed speech and excessive enthusiasm. Her hair hadn't been gray and thinning then; instead, it was glossy brown, with tumbling curls she was quite proud of. Her deep blue eyes rarely met others and were always downcast—an outcome of her childhood. Preferably, the dead never demanded eye contact or hollow conversations about the weather or upcoming holidays.

She continued to look at him, bewildered. He stood for some time with his hand outstretched awkwardly. His smile faded. His hand withdrew and so did he.

"Sorry! I can see you have plenty to do." He smiled again and left.

Once he'd retreated, she found herself wishing she had said something—*anything*. Why was this so hard? She tried to make an effort over the next few months. He was consistently warm and friendly to her, and in return she would smile and say, "Good morning!" like the others did. If she made a cup of tea, she brought him one. He genuinely seemed interested in talking with her. Finally, after about a year of skirting around it, he approached her one Thursday.

"Fia, would you like to have a drink with me after work?" She didn't know what to do. Of course she wanted to, but this meant conversation. Long conversation. She wasn't sure she could pull it off. But she had never been asked for a drink before. How could she pass it up?

"Yes, that would be lovely," she replied. "But I can only do an hour." A whole hour? Why didn't she say half an hour?

"Me as well! An hour will be perfect."

They ventured out to the pub over the road after closing up. He bought her a shandy and they found a quiet corner. At first, she listened to him talk, grateful for his effort. He began to ask her questions. Although it felt strange at first, she answered them. She shared her experiences, her thoughts, even her opinions. His warmth was so comforting and foreign, making her more at ease than she had ever been.

"Fia, tell me about yourself." He made steady eye contact. No one had asked her this in years.

"There's nothing to tell."

He reclined in his chair and smiled coyly at her. "Now, I know that isn't true."

She took a deep breath. "I was raised in Smyllum Park Orphanage. It was a very nasty place. I can't really say why and what happened. I left at eighteen. I only had one friend there, really." She swallowed hard. Just thinking about her brought it all back. Rory looked at her kindly.

"May I ask what happened to your parents?"

"I still don't really know. Different nuns would tell me bits and pieces of information. I think my mother died of some sort of illness. I was never really sure about my father. I have no memory of them."

Rory took a long drink of his ale. "Could you tell me about your friend?"

Fia could feel her throat tighten as she tried to say her name. It came out in a whisper.

"Hannah."

Even now, after all these years, her very name seemed to get caught in her throat. She remembered the chilling nights where they held each other under the covers, watching whisps of breath float up into the air. Fia was sure that there were times the cold might have killed them if they hadn't shared their warmth. She thought about the time Sister Martha locked her in the cellar, and Fia had been so hungry she considered grabbing one of the rats and stuffing it in her mouth. It had been Hogmanay that day, and as a very rare and special treat, the children were allowed outside to see a fireworks display. Her rumbling belly was drowned out by the crackles of fireworks and, somehow, Hannah had appeared in a flash, shoved some bread into Fia's bleeding hands, and disappeared again without a word.

Fia wouldn't be alive if it hadn't been for Hannah. She thought about these things, and then found herself telling Rory, "She was my dearest friend. My only friend, really. My family. But one night when we were both about seven or eight, I lay in my bed, waiting for her to appear. She had done something, I can't now remember what. I waited and waited. She never came. I thought perhaps she had been taken ill and was in the infirmary, but that really only happened if you were near to death anyway. I made the mistake of asking one of the nuns, who struck me just for asking. She never came back."

Rory reached across the table and took her hand. "Oh Fia. I am so sorry. Did you ever find out what happened to her?"

She couldn't quite believe this man was so interested in her sorry little life. She had carried these burdens for years. It felt wonderful to finally lay them down.

"No, not really. It wasn't until years later that they did a report on the place. It was years too late. But apparently children were buried there. Lots of them. None of the graves had stones or markers. I am assuming Hannah is there somewhere."

Rory hung his head, sharing in her sorrow, still grasping her hand.

"Thank you for telling me this, Fia."

It became their ritual. Every Thursday after work, they drank and chatted for their precious hour. It wasn't always so grim. She often found herself laughing and even teasing him at times. She began to count down the days until Thursday, soaking in his presence and conversation.

After a few months, they didn't part ways after the hour. Instead, they returned to the deserted funeral home. In the darkness, among the faded silk flowers and neutral paint colors, she allowed him to know her as no one ever had. A further ritual she anticipated with fervor.

Deep emotions that had been lost inside her resurfaced. She surrendered herself to them. And him. She let herself feel connected to another living human for the second time in her life. A future materialized before her, complete with a predictable terraced house, a garden, and a cat. Possibly even . . . a child.

One summer, unseasonable sweltering heat engulfed Glasgow. She had some vacation time to use and figured she would take a trip to the seaside—something else she had never done. She thought about asking Rory to accompany her, but it seemed a bit soon for that. Alone, she boarded the bus going to Lunderston Bay and rented a private room in the town center.

Having forgotten which day of the week it was, she wandered down to the seafront one Saturday morning as crowds began to gather. She removed her shoes and felt warm sand beneath her toes—another first. She heard and saw an ice cream truck. Perhaps she should treat herself.

As she joined the gathering queue, her attention was stolen by a gorgeous blonde in a cherry-red bathing suit in the distance. Two young ginger-haired boys were with her, although she wasn't sure of their ages. The youngest was still a toddler. Returning her gaze to the person in front of her, she noticed he was oddly familiar. Not noticing her at all, he ordered and paid, taking his tray of four ice creams. As he turned, she knew him immediately.

Suppressing an audible gasp, her eyes followed him as he walked toward the blonde bombshell and her sons. No, *their* sons. Now she knew where the ginger hair had come from.

"Miss?" asked the boy in the ice cream truck. "Miss? What can I get for you?"

She tore her eyes from the proverbial trainwreck, mumbled something, and left. Hot tears streamed down her face as she fled the beach.

She holed up in her room, returning to Glasgow earlier than planned. First thing Monday morning, she turned in her notice. She had little savings, but staying was not an option. She informed her landlady and began to pack. Her possessions were humble and few; packing did not take long. She planned to buy a bus ticket when another thought came to her.

She would rent a car instead. There was a detour southeast that had become necessary. She threw her belongings into the trunk and drove thirty miles to the place she had vowed never to return, stopping only for petrol on the way.

Wandering the grounds, she thought of Hannah. She wished she could conjure up a beautiful stone and lay it here in her memory. Instead, she had a different plan, which she carried out quickly and then returned to the car as darkness fell. A faint orange glow fell on the car as the flames engulfed her place of torture. No one was around. No one had seen her.

She wished to God she could burn up her memories in a similar fashion.

The journey north on the A90 was long and interminable. She returned the car and boarded the ferry to Lerwick, where passengers were tossed and battered around by the bitter North Sea. As she fought waves of seasickness, she reflected on all that had happened. After seeing his wife and family, she failed to comprehend how he had been interested in her, of all people? Was it all a cruel prank? Humiliation consumed her.

Upon her arrival, she sought the nearest funeral home and applied for a job, found lodging, and settled into communing once again with the dead, leaving the living to themselves. She checked the papers for years, following the story of the mysterious arson attack on Smyllum Park. To her good fortune—which in itself was unfamiliar—there were a series of similar attacks using petrol as an accelerant in both Lanarkshire and Ayrshire. Police had failed to detect any disparities in the attacks.

Years disappeared on the island, and when the time came to retire, she had a decision to make about where that would be. Somewhere remote. A place where she could be free of social obligation. A place she would never be found.

Angus's cottage now loomed up in the distance, and thankfully she could see his car in the drive. She exchanged brief pleasantries as she took his keys. He asked about her plans for Hogmanay, and as usual, didn't await her answer and instead told her about his own.

Again, she wondered if she should mention the child. Could he help her somehow?

She listened to his extensive plans and thought no, this was her problem.

She drove to Fort William. In Morrisons, she stood in the baby aisle. Nappies, soothers, formula, thousands of baffling pouches, bottles, wipes. What on Earth would she need?

She grabbed an array of things, along with a cheap pair of spectacles, and drove back to the loch. Slowly and carefully, she loaded the wagon, thankful Angus wasn't around then to ask questions. She pushed his keys through his letterbox and began the long journey back.

Rain was now falling, and she pulled her rain jacket snug around her. She tried to move quickly, as she knew the child didn't have long. Could she nurse it back to health? She wasn't sure, but she should at least try.

Trickles of water turned into rivers, making her walk back

even more arduous. There was no carved path to follow, but she knew these woods as she knew herself. Taking advantage of her knowledge, she found higher ground, but it meant adding more time.

As she traversed the difficult terrain, the child's sunken face kept returning to her, haunting her, as if it was shouting for Fia to hurry.

The wagon's wheels squelched in the thickening mud, and Fia used all her remaining strength to pull it through. Her garments were sopping, and she could feel the cold creeping in. Still, she trudged on, afraid to pause for even a moment's rest.

At last, the stony gray outline of the bothy appeared in the distance. A final burst of energy coaxed her through the last leg. She maneuvered the wagon inside, closed the door behind her, and went over to the drawer. She dried her hands and tried to warm them before touching the still body of the child.

She was cold.

She lit a fire and changed into dry clothes, draping the wet ones on an empty chair.

In her armchair, Fia sat and desperately tried not to remember feelings from the past. Behind the decadent flames and pinpricks of distant fireworks, ghosts of the past seemed to whisper. Her breathing quickened, and she glanced over to where the child lay.

Oddly, she found the presence of the dead, once again, to be of comfort.

Oh, how she wished it could be different.

She gave herself a sliver of permission to think about Rory, just for a moment. Was he still alive? Or lost to her from this world as so many others were? She wiped away a stray tear.

Thankful she had kept her tools and items for posterity, she prepared to embalm her. She fashioned a small coffin with some pine from the woodpile and filled it with heavy stones before gently lowering her inside. She carried it to the loch. After removing her wellies and socks, she stood for a moment as a hushed song escaped her lips.

For auld lang syne, my Dear,
For auld lang syne,
We'll tak a cup o' kindness yet,
For auld lang syne

"Auld Lang Syne." Times long past. She stepped into the icy shallows, walking until it was up to her waist. With sorrow, she pushed it out into the open, glassy water. It hovered above its reflection before gradually disappearing underneath the surface.

On the edge of the loch, on the trunk nearest to the water's edge, she set to work. Carving, inscribing, memorializing. Tiny shards of wood fell as sweat dripped off her forehead. She shivered from the cold and the wet but didn't step back to see her work until it was finished.

Hannah.

A gravestone for the graveless.

About the Author

Sharon Thatcher lives near the snow-capped mountains of beautiful British Columbia with her husband, daughter, and two cats. Although she has been writing for years, it's only recently she mustered up the courage to be bold and share her work. She is an English teacher who has lived and taught in both Canada and in the UK. A voracious reader, she loves to lose herself in stories both fictional and real.

She is currently enrolled in Curtis Brown Creative's incredible Writing Your Novel course, and she hopes to eventually finish up and publish her historical fiction novel.

You can find Sharon on:
Instagram @sharonthatcherbooks

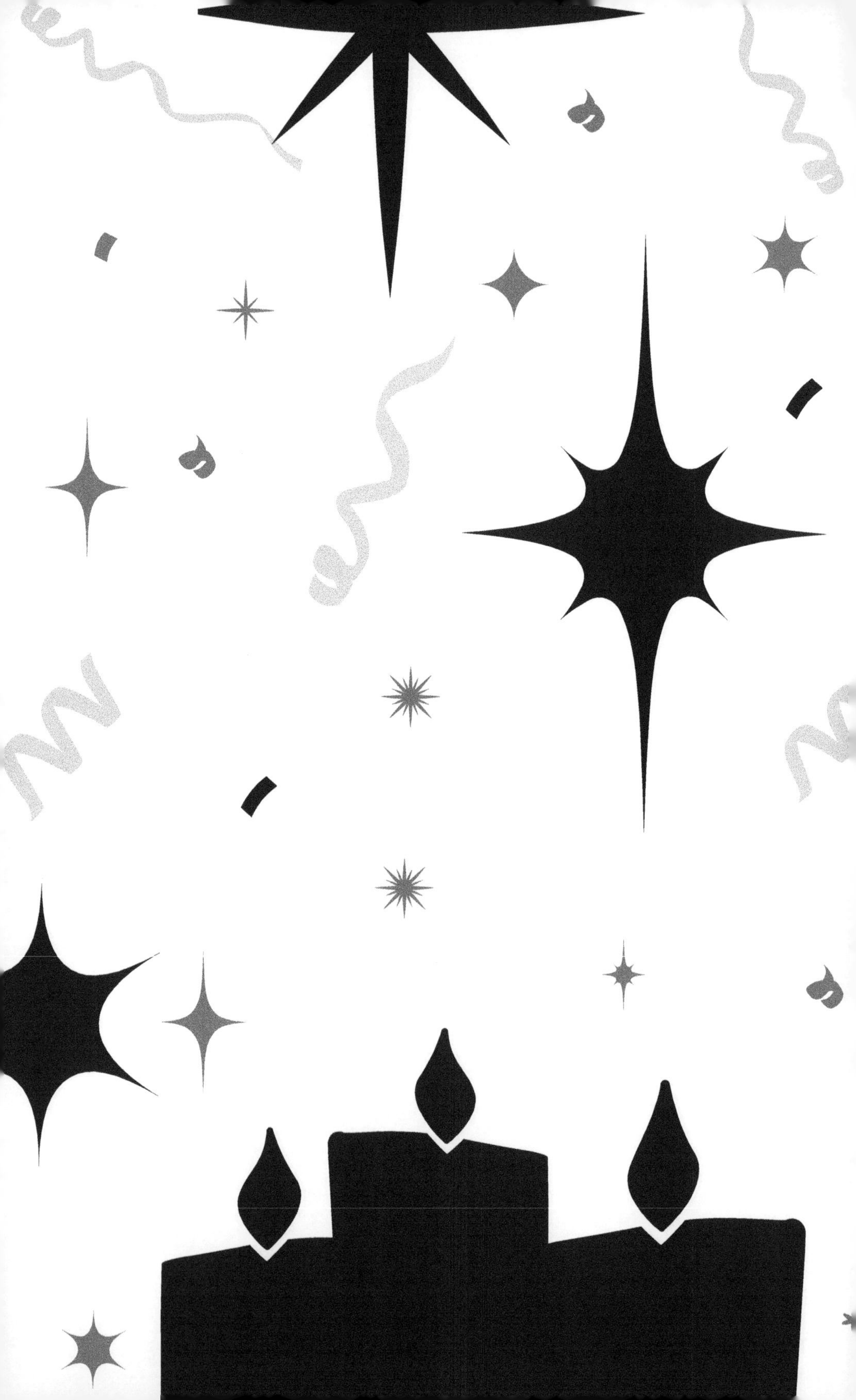

DANCING QUEEN

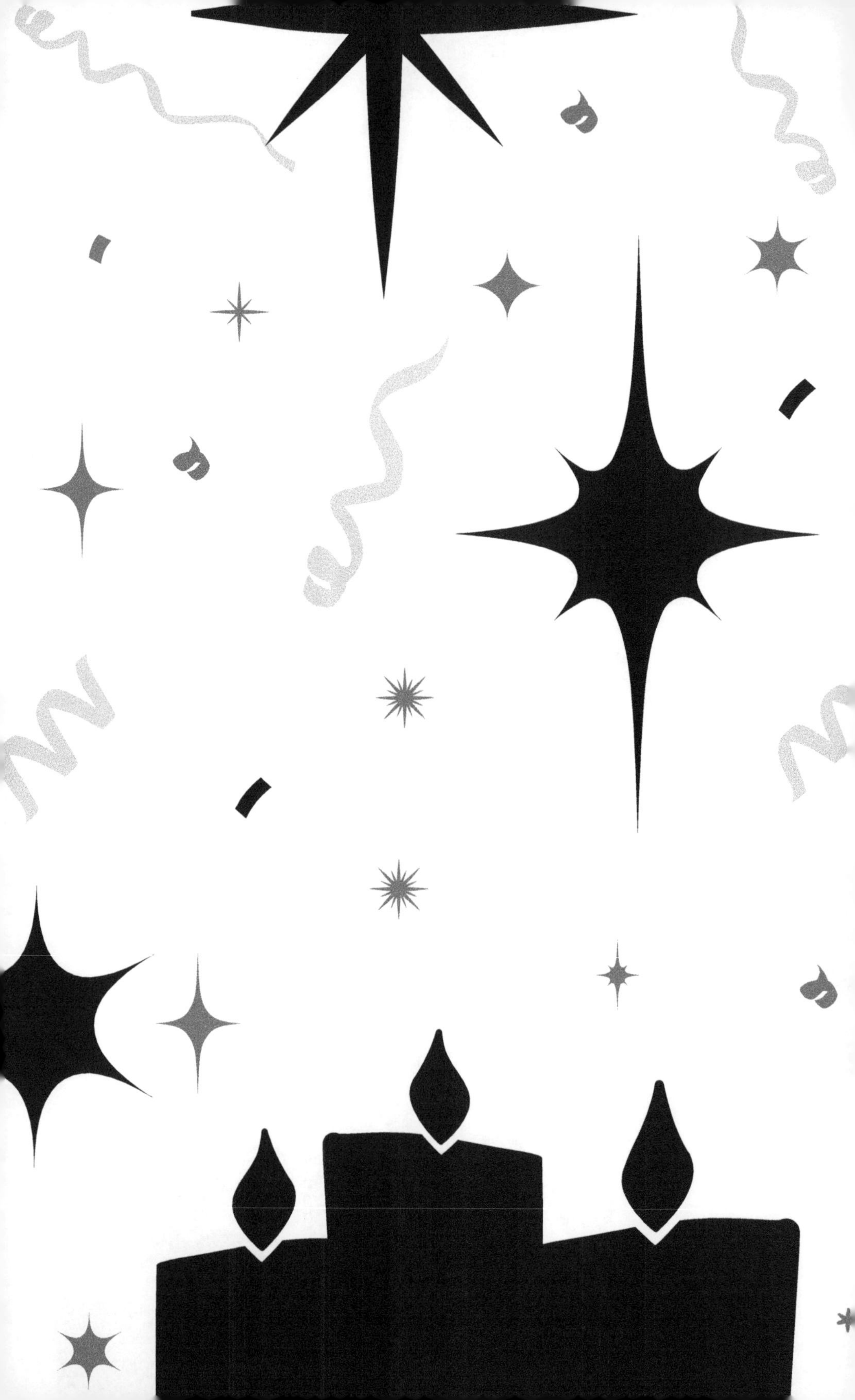

Dancing Queen

Jessica Daniliuk

QUINN WAS GOING TO END the year the same way it began: at the club waiting for a stranger to ask for a midnight kiss. She would stand by the bar, order herself a few drinks until someone worked up the courage to ask her to dance, and then decide if they were New Year's kiss material.

This proved to be foolproof in the past, so there was no way it wouldn't work now. It had to.

Quinn squeezed past a group of twenty-somethings and eventually made her way to the bar. She had never seen the club so busy; last year was child's play in comparison. Quinn saw this as her place since she had been here every Saturday night for the past three years. She'd go to the bar, nod at Frank, and he would make her usual to start off the night. But on this night, she was shoulder to shoulder with people she had never seen before, and it was seven minutes before she even made eye contact with Frank, never mind had a drink in her hand.

After the chaos of last year, Quinn had made a New Year's resolution that she would never find herself in a club on December 31 again. But . . . she was never one to keep New Year's resolutions on account of thinking they were stupid, so once again, Quinn found herself pushing through the crowd to get to her spot: a corner booth with a small table furthest away from the entrance.

This was the perfect place for Quinn to watch everyone and make predictions about their lives. In front of her were three young girls dancing together, belting along to "Dancing Queen." With an untrained eye, they looked like three friends having fun right before the start of a new year. But Quinn knew the truth—she was once all three of them. The first friend was a hopeless romantic, imagining she would find the love of her life on the dance floor tonight and they would have a magical kiss at midnight. She was singing with her friends, but her eyes were scanning the room for potential loves of her life. The second girl seemed a bit shy; the only reason she was dancing was because her friends were. She could be a really fun time, but only if someone pulled it out of her. The final girl was the one Quinn related to most. She was singing the loudest and dancing the proudest and no one would ever think she wasn't having fun, which was exactly the plan. If you go the extra mile and act like it's the best night of your life, no one will ask you if you're okay and you won't have to lie. The three girls continued dancing while Quinn took a long sip of her drink.

"Don't consider yourself a dancing queen?"

Quinn turned and was met with a striking pair of blue eyes.

The only thought that allowed itself into her head was *This is perfect midnight-kiss material.*

He got closer, and Quinn stayed right where she was. She realized it had been a minute and she hadn't actually said anything to the man.

"Not particularly. You?"

He grinned. Either he had already tried this line on five other women, and they had all given the same response, or he never thought someone would flip the question on him. For the first time in a while, Quinn wanted to find out.

"Maybe once when I was young, sweet, and seventeen, but after a couple years, I fear I've lost my funk."

Quinn felt a laugh bubble up.

"I'm Peter." He reached a hand out to her, but Quinn did not take it. She thought of a fake name to give him but kept it to herself.

"Quinn."

He smiled slightly so she could see some of his top teeth and none of the bottom. She finished her drink, wondering if he was waiting for her to say something or if he would continue the conversation.

Quinn was no stranger to being drunkenly hit on at the bar. If you went to one of the most popular clubs in the area every weekend and were the solid 8 that Quinn believed herself to be, you were bound to get some male attention. At times it was very unwanted, and Quinn would pretend she saw someone she knew and make a very clever and gracious exit. Other times, Quinn would find herself in a situation where the attraction was very one-sided—her being the one side. She would playfully make fun of the man until he had to verbally say he was not interested.

But with Peter things already felt different. She had no desire to put some scheme into action and also didn't care that he was taking his time to answer her. She had known this man for a mere three minutes but felt comfortable in the silence that hung between them.

"Why would a pretty girl like yourself be here all alone?"

And there it was.

Quinn felt that familiar pit in her stomach that told her it was time to get away and go somewhere else. Suddenly, there was a friend she had to meet.

"Sorry, that sounded very creepy and borderline disgusting. I promise I'm not a serial killer, which I know sounds like the least convincing thing ever. What I'm trying to say is you're beautiful and I would love to spend some time with you tonight."

The pit subsided. Quinn looked at his chest to see it raising and settling at an alarming rate. A bead of sweat passed by his icy-colored eye and raced all the way to the bottom of his chin. Quinn never found herself paying attention to these minute details before, but she was drawn to something about him. She was unimpressed by the original comment but admired his correction.

"You don't hit on women much, do you?" Playful banter was what she needed in the moment; it was familiar, safe.

"Was it the first attempt at a line or the apology that made it obvious?" He smiled again, wider this time, showing more teeth.

Quinn smiled back, staring at his lips. "Would it destroy all of your confidence if I said both?"

"Only slightly."

A small laugh escaped Quinn.

Peter inched even closer, and Quinn could smell the aftershave on him and felt the slight brush of his pants against her leg.

"Do you want to dance?" She surprised herself with the invitation; it had just slipped out.

"Just warning you for a second time, I'm no dancing queen." And yet, he held out his hand again.

Quinn took a deep breath and accepted.

They made their way to the dance floor past the three girls and many other enthusiastic partiers. Quinn wasn't the only regular at the club for New Year's Eve celebrations; she recognized a few other dedicated patrons she had grown used to seeing each week.

Roy was one of them, and every week he would request a Bon Jovi song and sit at the bar until they finally played it. When they did, he would clear a spot on the dance floor and perform a perfect impression of a fish flopping on a deck. Quinn could never tell if the impression was intentional or unfortunately spot on. Those who were not in attendance each week would look at Roy with a concerned, sometimes disgusted expression. Quinn always found a beauty in Roy's dance moves. He was fifty-three years old, dancing in a club full of twenty-somethings, not caring at all what they thought—just having the time of his life.

Quinn could never dance like that, not even in her wildest dreams.

As Peter and Quinn found an empty spot to call their own, the DJ transitioned from a new-aged pop song into "You Give Love a Bad Name." Quinn started to chuckle, excited to see how the New Year's Eve crowd would react to the artistic stylings of Roy. She looked over at his stool and, like clockwork, he started the routine. Quinn preemptively pushed Peter back and started cheering for Roy, who blew her a kiss and started flopping.

The young people around Roy began to snicker to their friends, eyebrows raised.

Quinn hesitantly turned to look at Peter. He had the widest smile Quinn had seen at that point, bottom teeth and all. He began cheering for Roy alongside Quinn, which caught Roy's attention. Roy motioned for the two to join, but Quinn shook her head. It was one thing to cheer and become excited by Roy's routine; it was another to get sucked into it and make a fool out of herself as well. She was happy to watch from the sidelines.

Briefly, she felt a hand on her shoulder before she was nudged slightly to the side. Without fully processing what was going on, Quinn now saw two fish: Roy and Peter. She released a noise she never expected herself to make. A laugh of pure joy and surprise she hadn't emitted in decades—perhaps since she was a little girl eagerly opening presents on Christmas morning. She clapped even louder, causing those around her to grow excited by proxy and cheer on the two men.

Fortunately or unfortunately, depending on who you ask, it was the fastest rendition of "You Give Love a Bad Name" Quinn had ever heard. The music transitioned into a new, more current song that proved to be of no interest to Roy. He gave Peter a quick hug, and when Peter's back was turned, gave Quinn a thumbs-up—his way of showing approval.

Peter made his way back over to Quinn, sweat stains on his collar and armpits and a clear lapse in his breathing. Quinn didn't know what to say; there was simply too much.

"That was truly . . . something," she screamed over the music.

Somehow his eyes were wider and bluer than before. "That was one of the most exhilarating things I've done in a while. Weirdly cathartic."

"It's the Roy way."

"Oh, that's his name. Good. It was gonna be awkward when I tried to make the 'What Would Roy Do' T-shirt without a name."

Quinn's shoulders raised as she laughed. Peter took a step closer; she could feel the post-flop heat radiating off his body. Every part of her wanted to kiss him, but it wasn't yet midnight.

"Do you want another drink? I'll get you one."

He looked genuine. She really wanted to trust him.

"I'm all set, thank you. But you can go grab one, and I'll wait here."

He mouthed *okay* and disappeared into the crowd.

Quinn tapped her foot along to another new-aged song she didn't know the words to. Yes, she'd been here every weekend, but she'd never bothered to learn the music that played most often. She'd thought knowing it would be pathetic. The people next to her knew the words. The guy whispered the lyrics into the girl's ear, but she didn't seem to mind. If anything, she liked it. They grew closer with each beat until they became one unit. A large blob of lust masquerading as enjoyment for the song. Quinn usually laughed at these couples, knowing that next week she would see him in here with a new girl. But tonight, she merely watched and withheld her judgement. She simply hoped they'd have a happy new year.

She heard the dancing queens shouting loud above the hum of the crowd: "One minute till midnight!" She located them among the bouncing and shuffling bodies easily just in time to catch the three of them take a shot and cheer afterward.

The couple next to Quinn started making out, apparently unable to wait until midnight. Quinn looked around, but there was no sign of Peter. She spotted Roy sitting on his favorite stool, chatting with the lady on the stool next to him. The music began to swell, and Quinn could feel it climb from her feet to her thighs. Everyone around her began yelling.

"Ten!" The music made its way to her ears. It wasn't the worst song she'd ever heard; she could learn the words if she wanted to.

"Six!" The couple hadn't stopped making out to participate in the bar's countdown, believing that getting to second base was more important. Quinn had to turn away.

"Three!" It seemed to Quinn like the bar was more crowded than ever, like more people had come inside just to say they rang in the New Year having fun. When Quinn retold the story of the night to her sister, she would be one of those people who had fun.

"One! Happy New Year!"

Quinn's corner booth called for her, and she badly wanted to answer.

She began to push her way past the crowd when she felt a slightly sweaty hand wrapped around her wrist.

"I'm so sorry I'm late—"

She grabbed his collar and pulled him in close.

Fireworks.

About the Author

Jessica Daniliuk is a writer from the Boston area. She recently graduated from the University of Massachusetts Lowell with a degree in Creative Writing. Through her studies, she has grown to love writing various forms of realism and even began experimenting with horror. She has previously been published in *The Offering* as well as the *Sigma Tau Delta Rectangle*.

You can find Jessica on:
Instagram @jmdaniliuk

Visit her website at https://www.jessicadaniliuk.com/

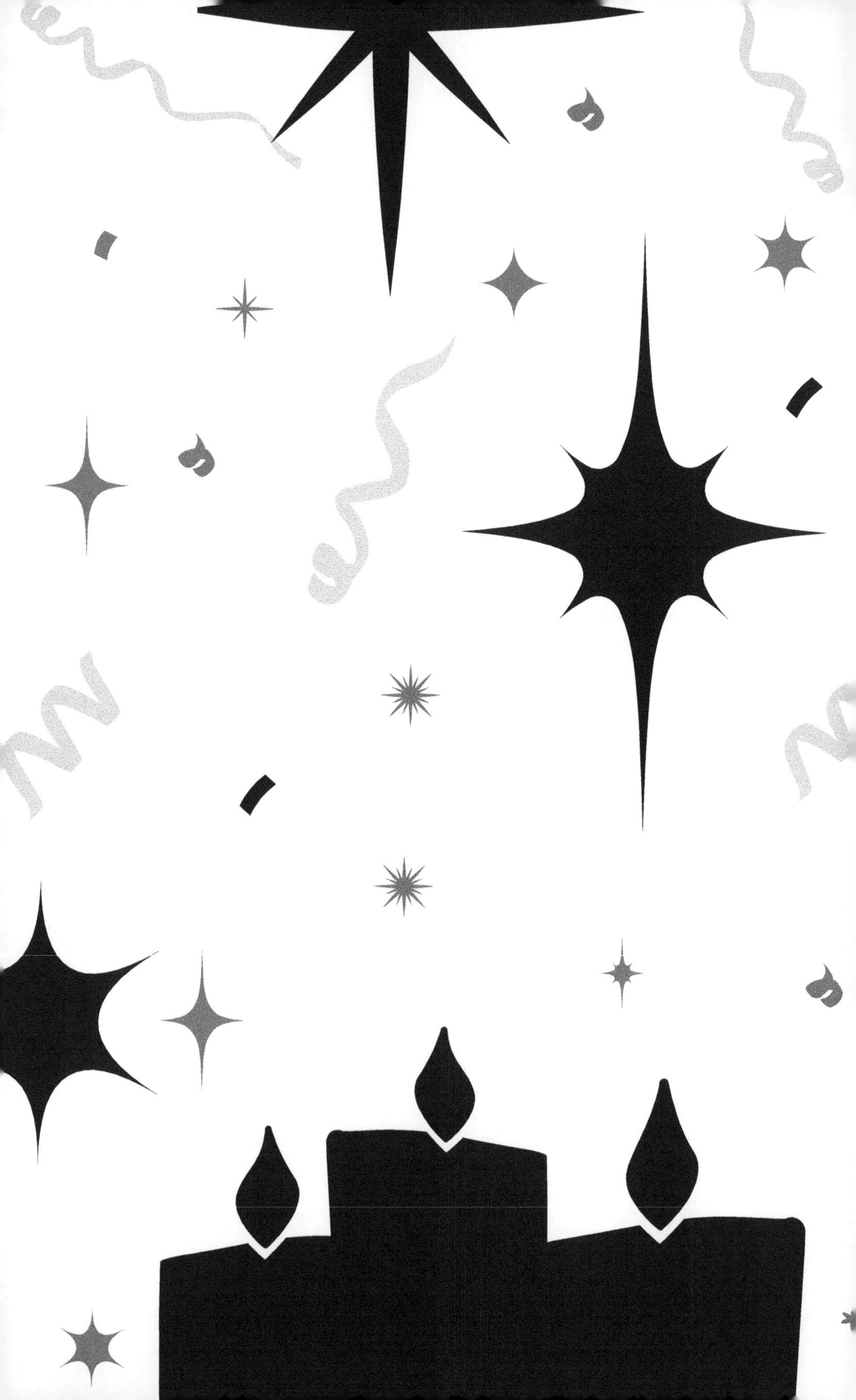

I'LL BE HOME FOR NEW YEAR'S?

I'll Be Home for New Year's?

Krista Renee

Chapter 1

Ella

EVERYONE WANTS TO HAVE A baby born on New Year's. Hell, people literally try to time their pregnancies around New Year's. Let me be the first to say what every person involved in Labor and Delivery is too scared to say: New Year's friggin' sucks. Or at least *this* particular one was shaping up to.

Not only did I have a set of twins scheduled for a C-section on New Year's, but two women had already gone into labor at almost the exact same time and it wasn't even technically New Year's Eve yet. Seeing my wife for midnight wasn't going to happen unless a serious miracle occurred. And at the moment, I needed a miracle—and fast.

I rolled my neck and changed out of my scrubs. The past year had been wonderful. I had more patients than I ever did in Houston. Mom, my current business partner, was letting me look for another doctor to take her place when she retired. A house of our own was being built on Momma's land. (Momma, my mother-in-law, not to be confused with *my* mom.) But my favorite moment was when Luella Anabeth Hutchinson said, "I Do."

After everything we've been through, the lingering fear of her leaving no longer played on repeat in my brain—and hadn't for some time. She was my wife, my partner, my lover, mine. Out of all my accomplishments, our love story was my favorite.

While I waited on the water to heat up, my fingertips ran along my belly. As an OBGYN, I knew all the rules that came with trying to get pregnant. The first being not to get your hopes up. So many things could go wrong. Especially the first time. But the part of me that had Lu's DNA in my womb really hoped it took.

I knew the irony of me before we got married, versus me now. Not wanting kids used to be my personality trait. Now I had the chance to have something that was both me and Lu. I'd have been an idiot to not jump on the chance.

We had two days before I could test. Two days of hell. I was nauseous as all get-out and my boobs had been aching for a week. If that wasn't the biggest neon sign of my life, I didn't know what was.

"Dear baby, if you're in there, please stick. Momma really wants to meet you. And she deserves happiness. If you stick, I promise you'll have more love than you'll ever know what to do with."

After my shower, I changed into a clean pair of scrubs and messaged Lu.

Happy New Year, Mrs. Young. I miss you.

She took a total of thirty seconds to respond. Guess I wasn't the only one not sleeping. *It's barely New Year's Eve, Doctor Young. I miss you too. Do your boobs feel any better?*

Nooope. Which is making me miss you more. Come teleport to me.

You know, I'd love to. Unfortunately, I'm enjoying my cozy bed. On the plus side, it'll be warm when you get back.

You're a dick.

I knew the exact smile that crossed her face when she texted her response: *But I'm your dick.*

Yes. Yes you are.

I know you aren't supposed to test yet, but maybe we can take it at midnight? Is one day gonna make that much of a difference?

I should've told her we needed to wait. The logical part of me knew that. When it came to Luella Anabeth Hutchinson-Young, logistics flew out the window. In a perfect world, we'd lay in bed all day.

Do you want the doctor's answer, or your wife's answer? Because they aren't the same.

Oh, come on! You wanna know, too! You haven't gotten your period yet, your boobs are sore. Not to mention peanut butter is making you want to vomit. It's one day, doctor.

I chewed on my cheek. I laid on the hospital bed and drummed my fingers on my stomach. She was right and she knew it. *If I agree, sugar, which I'm haven't, but if I do, it could come out negative.*

But it could turn out positive.

Fineeeeee. If these two babies aren't born by midnight, come to the hospital and we'll take a test. At the very least, we'll get to spend midnight together.

I love you, Eleanor Lennox Young.

Not as much as I love you, Luella Young.

I kicked my feet with a squeal. Lu had my last name. I'd never get tired of saying it. She was mine.

Chapter 2
Lulu

I PACED THE EMPTY DINER at 9:00 a.m. We had less than twelve hours before we found out if Ella was pregnant. I knew the list of things that could go wrong. And trust me, there were a lot. I'd been pregnant. But my heart told me she was pregnant. I really hoped my heart was right.

A blast of cold air hit me in the face when the door opened.

"Morning, Lu!" Jill Young said.

I stopped pacing long enough to give her a small smile. Jill was back in Ella's life. Kind of. And it wasn't like she was bad . . . in theory. But she also happened to be sleeping with Momma, and my brain was having a rough time processing it. If they got married, Ella and I would be stepsisters. While Ella and I were planning our wedding when they got together, I didn't want to imagine the looks our kids got when other kids found out their grandmothers were screwing.

Was it wrong to say I hoped they didn't ever marry each other?

"Morning."

Momma came out holding a pie. Her eyes lit up when they locked on Jill.

I sank into the middle stool and banged my head on the counter. So much for them keeping it low key. *Damn it, Ella, why are you never here when I need you?*

"Where's Ella?" Momma asked while she put the pie in the

case. "I thought she'd be spending your first New Year's as newlyweds with you."

Cue me banging my head on the counter again. Ever since she hooked up with Jill, Momma wasn't great at reading the room.

"'Cause I just enjoy spending New Year's alone," I muttered as I lifted my head. "She had to work."

I side-eyed Jill when she sat beside me. "Good thing I'm retiring, huh, peaches?"

Ella was the one who was hopefully pregnant, but I was the one who suddenly had the overwhelming urge to vomit.

Momma smiled at me, and I couldn't help but pout. I was married, and life was good, but dang, I missed when Momma was mine. Not Jill's. Mine.

She gave my hand a squeeze. "Maybe she'll get off before midnight."

I exhaled loudly. "Even if she did, she'd have to be at the hospital in the morning."

Sammy's fingers gave my shoulders a squeeze. I leaned into him and closed my eyes. He might've not said much, but I'd always be thankful for his quiet comfort. As far as co-owners of diners went, he was my favorite . . . second favorite, Momma was my favorite. He leaned next to my ear and whispered, "She'll make it home, Lu."

I sure hoped he was right.

At noon, I hugged my knees to my chest. Aside from Momma and Jill's cars, the parking lot was bare. "Guess everyone's too busy celebrating with their families."

My phone dinged. *One baby out, three to go!*

Maybe Sammy was right. Maybe, just maybe, Ella would be home for New Year's.

Chapter 3
Ella

DID I SELL MY SOUL IN exchange for three women to get to ten centimeters within minutes of each other? No. But whatever god was out there was my new favorite person.

I ran from the first room into the next. A strange rush of giddiness soared through my veins when my patient's legs were in stirrups, and she was ready to push.

It was five-thirty. Depending on how long this delivery took, it was possible Lu would be in my arms at midnight. "Dear god," I whispered. "Please let this delivery go smoothly."

And it did.

Luck must've been on my side, because at six, the baby had made her big debut. By seven-thirty, the twins were being examined. All in all, New Year's Eve in L&D hadn't been as bad as I'd anticipated.

Regardless of whether the test came back positive, I was going to celebrate with my wife. She would always be worth the exhaustion. She was worth everything. And there was one thing I had to do before I went home.

I stopped by the store and got a bouquet of flowers and a bottle of sparkling cider. After sending her a kissy face emoji, I headed back to Sulphur Bluff, to the only woman I've ever loved. Even before we were a couple, Lulu had been my home. Nothing made sense without her.

After I parked in our driveway, I sat on the hood of my car and watched the cotton candy sky fade to black behind our future home. Next year, we'd ring in the New Year on our porch. I wanted to scream that nothing would top this year, but every year I was with her was going to be better than the previous. *Lucky* didn't begin to describe what I was or how I felt.

A car pulled in beside me. I stretched and slid off my hood. I didn't know what was more unsettling: my mom standing next to my car smiling at me, or my nausea. One hand rested on my belly, while my other attempted to massage the knots in my back.

"Mom?"

She wrapped her arm around my shoulders and pulled me against her. "I'm so glad you're home. I have something to tell you."

My jaw clenched. Luck wasn't on my side anymore. Either she was telling me she was working in my office, or she found a place close to us. Neither of those options worked for me.

"Oh?"

She dragged me inside and pushed me on the couch. Another option crossed my mind, but I refused to allow myself to entertain it.

"Stay here. I gotta find your wife."

Yup. Option number three was shaping up to be my reality. In other words, I was screwed.

Chapter 4
Lulu

MOMMA AND JILL CORNERED ME while I was eating pie. Their smiles were wide. Too wide. It was the kind of smile a kid has when they're trying to hide something.

"I have a present for you, but you gotta follow me."

I groaned and looked at the pie. If I got up, I wouldn't be able to finish my pie. I didn't want to live in a world where I couldn't finish my pie. Nobody should live in a world like that. "Buttttt."

"Ella's home."

She didn't have to tell me twice. I followed Momma into the living room and jumped onto Ella with a squeal. "You're home! My wife's home!"

Her mouth was greedy when it met mine. I didn't care that our moms could see. Ella was home! That was all that mattered. I shooed them away when they cleared their throats. Nothing was gonna ruin this moment.

"We're getting married."

I guess even hell can freeze over. "Ella," I squeaked. "Did she just?"

"Yup."

I yelped when she threw me on the couch and rose to her feet. She approached her mother, her hands clenched into frustrated fists. "You always have to get the last word. Thank you for ruining finding out if I'm pregnant. You're friggin' wonderful."

"Sorry, Momma," I whispered, before running to find Ella.

I found her sitting on the porch with her knees to her chest. I sat behind her and kissed her neck. "At least our life won't be boring, doctor."

Her whole body shivered, and I had to fight a giggle. She sighed, still irritated by the news. "You realize them getting married makes us stepsisters?"

I braided her dirty blonde hair and sighed. "Yeah. . . . You smell sweet."

"I planned on changing, then that happened." Her bottom lip jutted. "I really wanted our first New Year's to be memorable."

"I meeean . . . it kind of has been."

She wrapped her arms around my torso and rested against my belly. "What am I gonna do with you, Luella Young?"

"I would say marry me, but you already did that. Sooooo, make a baby with me?"

I squealed when she wrapped my legs around her waist and carried me in the direction of our future home. "How about we play doctor and patient? I'm about to break so many rules."

Chapter 5
Ella

I PACED LU'S BEDROOM AT 11:59 p.m. "This is the longest three minutes of my friggin' life."

Lu counted down with a squeal. "Three... two... one... it's midnight! Flip it over."

My hands framed her face. I pressed my lips to hers, allowing myself to melt into her. Our foreheads rested against each other. "Positive or not, you're my favorite chapter."

"Good. Cause you're mine."

After a long exhale, I turned over the test. My hands shook so hard I almost dropped it. You'd think I've never held a pregnancy test in my life.

My mouth dropped. Not only were there two lines, but the second was bright. I was pregnant with a baby. Lu's baby. Golden brown eyes searched my face expectantly.

"Well?"

I turned it so she could see. Her yell was so loud it made our moms knock on the door and ask if we were okay.

"Pregnant?" she whispered. Tears flowed down her cheeks. "We're having a baby?"

I picked her up and spun her around. "We're having a baby, Lu!"

She sobbed into my shirt. In the four years we'd been together, she'd been pregnant by the worst man imaginable, but I also saw her put a hell of a lot of work in after. She'd grown into a strong woman, and this time getting pregnant was her decision. It hadn't been forced on her.

"You're having my baby."

I set her on the counter and kissed her beautiful tear-stained face. "I'm having your baby, Mrs. Young."

She wrapped her arms around my neck. "Happy New Year, Doctor Young."

I smiled and kissed her. Happy New Year, indeed.

Lulu and Ella are the main characters in Krista Renee's debut novel, **Bad Idea Lane**, *which released in 2024. To read more about them, pick up a copy today! Available in print and ebook on Amazon and other retailers.*

About the Author

Krista Renee writes sapphic romances ranging from sweet and sassy to dark and gritty. Her debut novel *Bad Idea Lane* came out in July of 2024, and she's currently working on a dark *Wizard of Oz* retelling. She lives in East Texas. When she's not obsessing over Broadway, she's hanging out with her four munchkins.

You can find Krista Renee on:
Instagram @kristareneeauthor
Facebook @kristareneeauthor

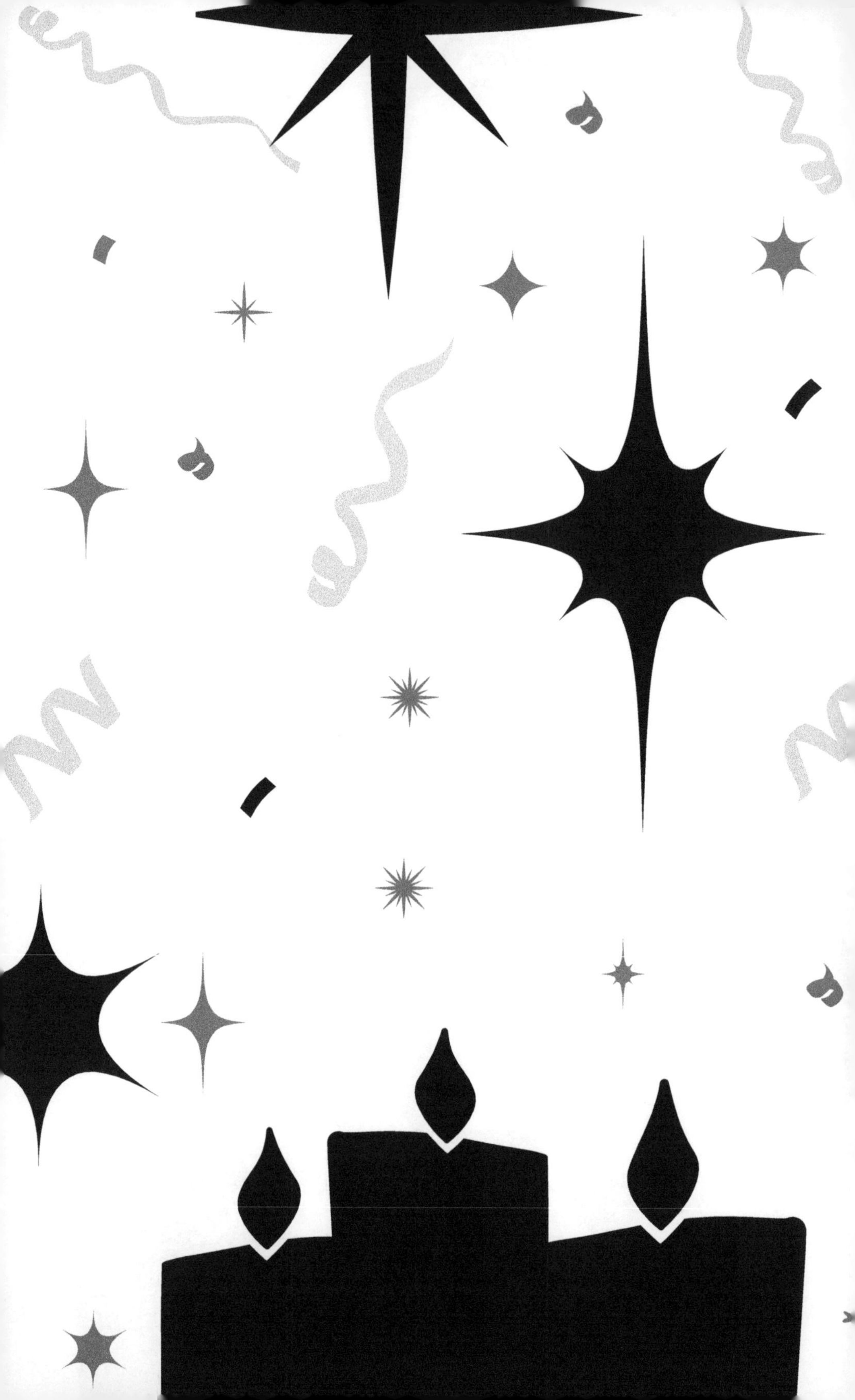

WHAT ONE WOULD DO FOR A ROSE

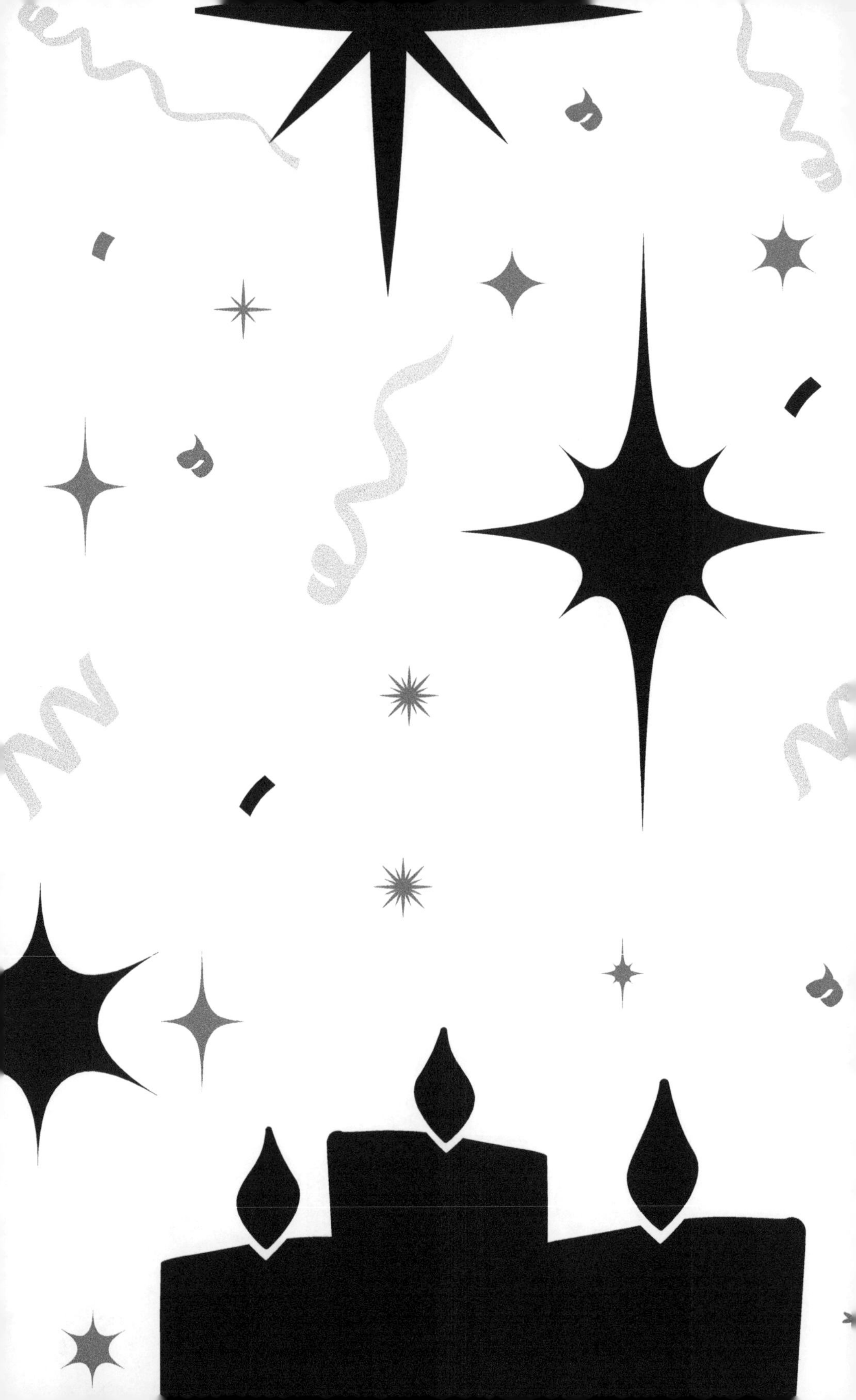

What One Would Do for a Rose

H. Buckley

"It is the time you have wasted for your rose that makes your rose so important."
—Antoine de Saint–Exupéry, *The Little Prince*

SNOW WALTZED AROUND GEORGE BEFORE gently kissing the ground and crunching under his black boots. Multicolored lights entangled themselves around oak trees like newfound roots. George wandered close to them, challenging the falling snow to a game of hide-and-seek. The snow won. He hid his face in a red tartan scarf, but the snow teased him and tickled his nose.

On any other day, he'd warm his hands and practice piano in the air, oblivious to the locals' perplexed looks. Alas, Christmas presents kept his hands occupied. Even so, his heart fluttered at the idea of mastering *La Campanella* for his next concert. He sighed, close to home, so close to the fire. A smile played on his face.

Turning toward his white Edwardian villa, he stopped to admire the glittery sheet of untouched snow resting in the front garden. It reminded him of his wedding day. Although the chilly night began freezing his toes, he ignored it to enjoy the scene for a moment longer. Blocks of snow glided off the roof, landing on the ground with a soft *thud*. They joined the white duvet, offering cold comfort to winter honeysuckles, camellias, and primroses who lay sound asleep.

Behind the villa, ripples from Seaton River complemented the silent symphony before him. In a way, it made the stack of gifts feel lighter. He inhaled the frosty air, and when he blew out the vapor, he imagined himself as a dragon ready to fly away with his family—destination: December 26, 2010, his wedding day.

Oblivious to his tranquil condition, the chilly temperature weighed the presents down. It forced his arms to shake, and the presents rattled. Misty Callander's sharp voice snapped him out of winter's enchanted state as the front door creaked open. "I give my all for this family, and what do I find? A God-awful man gawking like a lovestruck tart. Get inside before you freeze!" Snow crashed from the rooftop, and he apologized to the flowers before he rushed inside.

"How much have you spent? Don't lie to me," Misty said. She removed his scarf and brushed the snow from his thick black hair. Once satisfied, she tugged her silk shawl, and her honeycomb curls swayed back into formation. She had sculpted it to perfection, no strand unaccounted for.

"I lost the receipts. But trust me, we are making a profit." George flashed a well-rehearsed smile and rushed toward the living room.

"Are you kidding me? You know my credit card was declined at the wine club the other night. The girls are gossiping about me.

They think we're poor, George—*poor*," Misty said, close to tears.

George wasn't buying it. He'd known her long enough to spot the difference between misery and theatrics.

"You are always the topic of gossip, my doe, with or without a credit card. And what's the point if I'm rich but can't make her smile? You know how she loves gifts, and I bought extra to make up for being away. But don't worry. I've got you something just as wonderful."

George poked his head into the vast living room, Misty's complaints coasting through one ear and out the other. His heartbeat slowed as he gazed at his daughter, who knelt beside the ten-foot Christmas tree, playing with baubles, gold tinsel, and red beads.

"I've booked a table at that new restaurant tomorrow night, the one you said deserved a Michelin star. I pulled a few strings so they'd open for us even though it's New Year's Day. Don't worry about the details. I've got it all covered," George whispered, feeling proud of himself for the romantic gesture.

Misty gaped. "You know how expensive that place is—"

Sniffing, George interjected, "Do I smell something burning?"

Eyes wide, Misty dashed to the kitchen, and he chuckled at his own brilliance. But beneath that, he wished she'd expressed some appreciation for what he'd planned for them.

The aroma of roast turkey filled the house, but he felt the tension in his shoulders melt away when he caught the sweet scent of the cinnamon candles on the windowsill.

Unknown to George, however, the lit candles signaled passing friends that Misty yearned for company—but only those friends with the money who could bring her favorite Louis Roederer Cristal Champagne with them.

George tiptoed into the living room. The double-sided fireplace crackled as it ravenously ate the dry wood. On the limestone mantelpiece lay exquisite snow globes he'd found on tours abroad. To his left, the antique grandfather clock chimed seven o'clock. But the little girl continued pulling down decorations and playing. George considered flopping on the green armchair and warming his hands near the fire. Then, he would perfect *La Campanella* on his grand piano in the corner beyond the tree. But instead, he placed the gifts on the beige carpet and snuck behind her.

"Roar!" George grabbed his daughter and spun her around.

"Ah, your hands are cold," she squealed and climbed onto his back. "Do you like my tree?"

"You should do this every Christmas. Why don't you stay on my back and decorate the middle?" George shuffled the decoration box between his feet.

"Mummy said I had to take them down. But I can play with them if I'm very careful."

"Why would Mummy say that?"

"Because Christmas is over, and she wanted it gone for tonight."

"What's going on tonight?" George teased.

"Her party. She said I could stay up late if I behave."

"A party?" George furrowed his brows. Misty had never told him about a party.

Misty's heavy steps echoed across the cottage before George could ask for more details. "The food is burning. You're playing make-believe, and these presents are in my way!" She kicked the presents, and the smallest one fell with a crack. George spun, and his eyebrow twitched. Their daughter gasped and held the bauble in her hands so tight her knuckles went white.

"Sorry, darling, Mummy needs my help. Why don't I move the chair? You can stand on it and reach more baubles?" George asked.

He lifted her onto the armchair, rolled it next to the tree, and shouted, "Choo choo!" Her smile was infectious, and her eyes were beacons of fire that warmed his soul. But when he glanced at Misty, the warmth vanished.

Misty seemed to love frowning, and it left a mark even though she was young. He reached for the small gift, sniffling from the cold or her cruelty, he wasn't sure which.

"If you pick that up, I'll be gone by morning," Misty said. She glared at their daughter, who looked lost in thought with a gold ornament in her hand.

"Misty, my doe—"

"You heard me—"

"Let's talk in the kitchen. I'll help you cook," George said. He reached for her hand. She slapped it away. He felt like an anchor had pierced his heart and thrown him overboard into the deep blue sea.

Shuffling with his head low, George hoped to have an eloquent argument to appease Misty. But when he entered the kitchen, his mind froze, and he grimaced.

"Anna, why are you here? It's New Year's Eve. Why aren't you in Edinburgh with your family?" George turned to Misty, "And when were you going to tell me about the party?" he asked. Every countertop space was covered in gourmet appetizers, pastries, and finger foods. His stomach fluttered with excitement at the pigs in blankets.

"Olivia Mayfair agreed to pay my tab at wine club if we hosted this year," Misty shrugged.

"It's really no bother," Anna said. "I had no plans for New Year's, anyway," Heat flooded the room as Anna opened the oven, retrieving enough mini quiches to feed the street.

Misty snapped, not even bothering to look at the quiches.

"Well, don't expect me to pay you, burning everything for our guests. The ungratefulness! You're doing this on purpose, aren't you?" She slammed the oven shut. Anna flinched, causing two quiches to fall off the pan and onto the floor with a loud *splat*.

"No—"

"Don't lie to me."

"Misty, pipe down. Anna did nothing wrong," George said, then turned to Anna, whose lips trembled as sweat beaded her forehead. "I'll pay for your taxi and help tonight. If you're in luck, you'll catch the last train."

George paid Anna, and she apologized and left.

Meanwhile, Misty leaned against the oak table and fiddled with her cross necklace. A tear streamed down her porcelain face.

"Tell me what's wrong."

"Isn't it obvious?" Misty sighed, and for a moment, the theatrics turned to misery,

"No?" George breathed deeply, and his skin wrinkled around his brows.

"Why are you here?" Misty asked.

"I live here?"

"Do you? When was the last time we had a meal together?"

"I warned you about this, my doe. Christmas is busy."

"The ladies think I'm a single mother, you know. They think you're cheating. That you spent Christmas day with a model in Vienna, or London, or wherever you were. Do you even care about me? About our agreement?"

"Agreement? My doe, it's New Year's—"

"When we agreed to have a child," Misty began, hand raised, "I said yes under one condition: I don't raise the child alone. I compromised and asked for money to spend with my friends. Then you stripped me bare. Do you understand there are consequences? There are consequences to making me miserable."

"We also agreed we'd sacrifice for her. I canceled your card to get her gifts, as we agreed. I am trying to show her how much I love her." George sighed, flopped onto the yellow dining chair and ran his fingers through his hair.

"Are you sure about that?"

"Of course."

"What did she dream about last night?"

"What?" He stared into her siren-green eyes.

"Your daughter, the one you love. Tell me what she dreams about. Tell me one thing about her."

"I wasn't here—"

"You're never here—"

"I am." George clenched his teeth, and his face flushed red.

"Tell me what she dreams about!" Misty slammed her hands on the table. "She dreams about *you*. Do you hear me? She always dreams about you. About a father who is there for her. Who wipes her tears and kisses her bruises. She dreams about a man who doesn't slam the door every morning but stays and says, 'Rose, I'm here for you. I'll do anything for you'. She never stops dreaming about you!"

"I have no choice." George's blood boiled, but his voice remained steady. "I have to make a living, Misty. What will we do if I stop, huh? I don't enjoy being away from her. Playing piano is lonely without the person you love being there. But this is how it is. I'm not going to make us destitute because you're tired."

"Something has to change. Rose can't be fatherless forever."

"If you're so wise, what do you suggest? Do you have a plan, or will you just complain and run away?" George taunted, and Misty's tears turned into a tidal wave.

"Do you know what she asked Santa for Christmas?"

"Oh, give me a break."

"That you were *here*."

Silence invaded the room, cutting through bone and marrow with the pain of neglect. George stared longingly out the kitchen door, grieving for his daughter and how her mother had failed to prepare her for Christmas without him.

Misty wiped her moist cheeks. "But I have a plan this time."

"Spit it out then." He leaned back and crossed his arms.

"Your daughter, the one who wishes she knew you . . ." Misty inhaled a deep, shaky breath. "I want to send her to boarding school, the one my parents run in America. They'll take her for free until she graduates. She'll be smart, brilliant, everything you're not. Maybe she'll get into Harvard or Cambridge."

George shot daggers at her, holding back the urge to ask her how long it took her to master *Gaspard de la Nuit*.

"But most importantly," she continued. "Her grandpa will be her father, and she'll stay far away from you. You can't be *her father* until you're ready to be *my husband*. It's not fair. I won't have it any longer."

Misty slid her phone with the acceptance email across the oak table.

"She will not be thrown aside because her existence inconveniences you," George's voice broke. "We promised we'd make it work. Are you breaking your promise? Trust me. We can find another way. I love you. I spent hours finding the perfect gifts—"

"We don't want your gifts, George. We want you."

"Mummy?" Rose tiptoed from the hallway, head held low with the broken giftbox in hand. Misty spun around and away from Rose's innocent eyes.

"I slipped and fell on it. I didn't mean to make it worse," Rose handed George the gift, and he lifted her onto his knee. She shifted uncomfortably in his lap.

"Don't worry, my darling. We can fix it together. That's what families do, don't you agree?"

"If you're not willing to pay the cost, it's better left broken," Misty whispered.

George breathed deeply and began unwrapping the gift. "I paid a man in Vienna to create a music box with a sculpture on top. It's me and Mummy dancing together."

He lifted the music box to find Misty's head was broken. Rose gasped.

"Don't worry, we can fix it. You wind it up, and it plays a lullaby that we dance to. I hope it reminds you of our love for you, Rose."

George fiddled with the music box, and then it played a soft melody. Rose's eyes beamed with wonder.

"I must tell my teddy." Rose rushed off his lap.

They waited until she was out of earshot, both calculating their next move.

"You truly are a God-awful man." Misty turned. "Either you send her away, or I'm leaving both of you. I can't do this anymore. I can't keep wiping her tears because her father isn't coming home. Think hard, George. You can't play a sweet melody and expect the stars to align for you."

George reached for her hand. She slapped it away.

"What do you expect me to do with her? I'm supposed to play in Portugal next week, then Spain the week after. I can't cancel."

"Oh no, poor George is in a pickle. Is this the first time you've heard of sacrifice?" she mocked. "Six years, I've given her. It's your turn to play parent. You have till midnight."

A severe chill ran down his spine as Misty left the room,

muttering about how she needed to get ready for her party. Dizziness silenced his racing mind, unable to focus on anything but the cruel choice she'd set in front of him.

Upstairs, he heard Rose's light footsteps, no doubt retelling the story of how she'd received such an incredible gift. He held his head in his hands, feeling defeated, rejected, and powerless.

While the world kept turning, multitudes gathering to celebrate the end of the year and anticipate the joy of a new one, George sat frozen in the torment.

Tonight, he'd either lose his daughter to save his marriage or lose his wife to save his daughter.

A soft patter sounded on the staircase. He bottled up the tears as Rose raced for a hug. And with her tight in his arms, he wished he could cry out, but instead, he told her, "There's nothing I wouldn't do for you, my darling. I love you, always."

About the Author

H. Buckley, born in Croydon, is a graduate of the University of Aberdeen. Her poetry collection, *Theology in a Divided World*, took shape during lockdown, ignited by a policeman's murder of a woman fifteen minutes from her home—a tragedy that hit hard, and she often thinks, "That could have been me." This compelled her to write, finding in poetry a voice to confront the injustices that go unspoken or are forgotten too quickly.

In addition to writing, Buckley loves highland cows, coffee, and running, which lets her brain breathe and brainstorm new ideas—writing is always on her mind. As a Master's student in Creative Writing, she's committed to lifelong learning, seeing each piece she writes as a step forward. Her debut short story, "What One Would Do for a Rose," appears in this anthology, and her piece "In the Stillness" was a finalist in a competition with the Scottish Wildlife Trust. Buckley's journey has only just begun, and she's excited to keep learning and growing, one story at a time.

You can find H. Buckley on:
Instagram @h.buckley_author

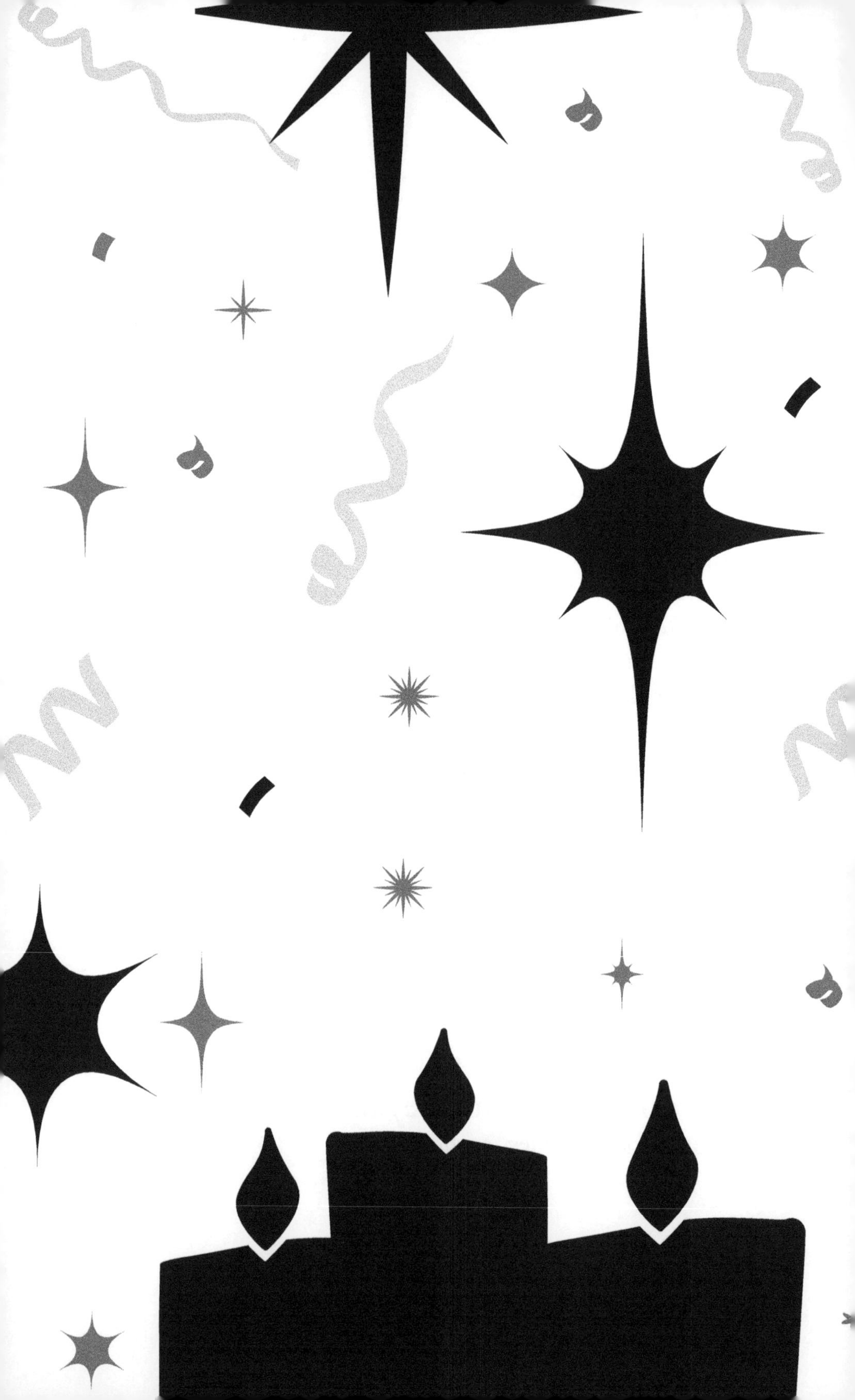

NEW YEAR'S BABY

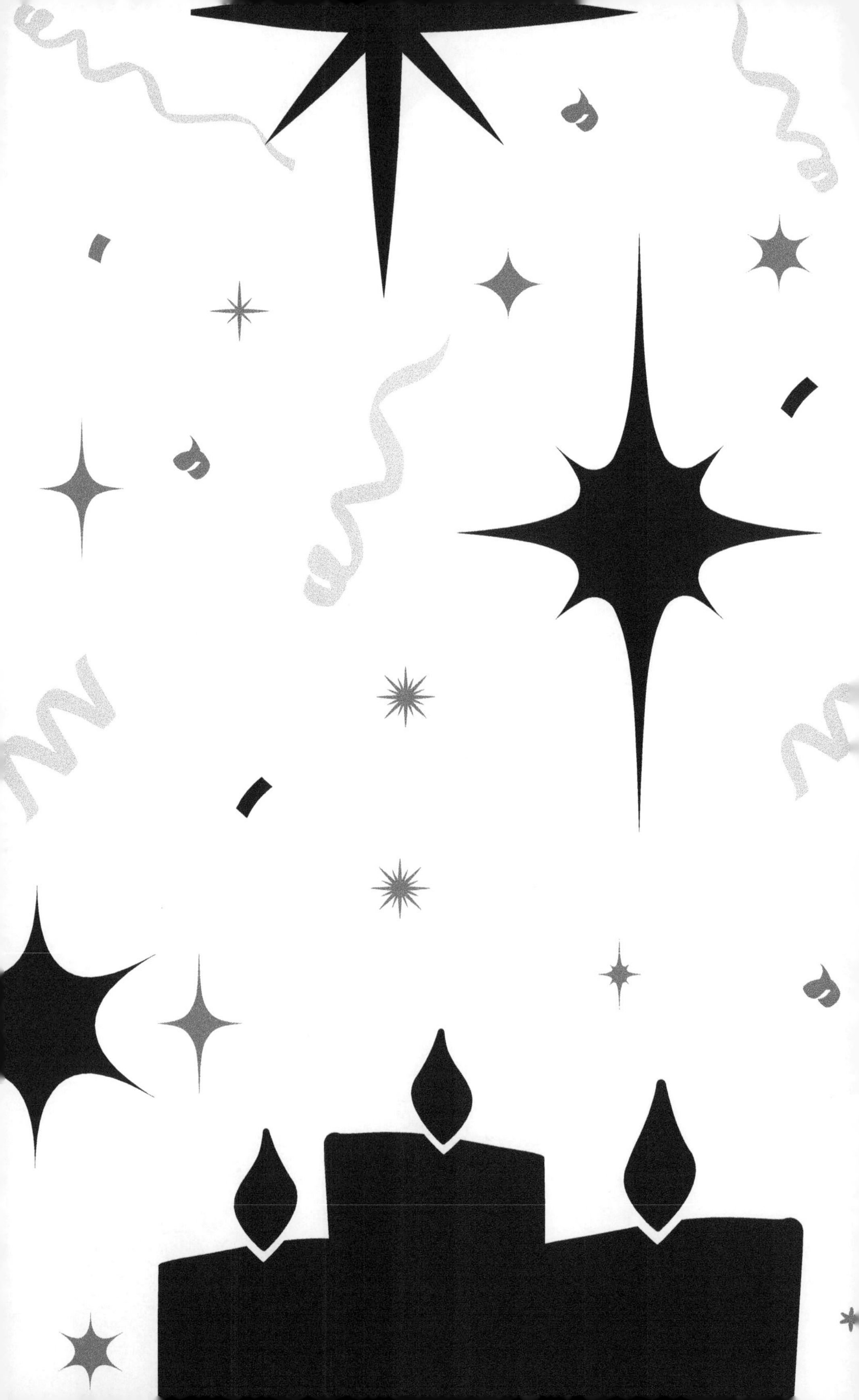

New Year's Baby

Anna Picari

DURING HER THIRTY-FIFTH WEEK appointment, Jennifer listened intently as her obstetrician said, "Since this baby is almost five pounds, I think we should discuss the possibility of an induction at thirty-nine weeks."

The second-time mother looked at her doctor and asked in a voice worthy of a more qualified, veteran mother, "That's right after Christmas. The baby isn't due until January seventh, and her sister was born eight days after her due date. Will her lungs be developed? Her brain? Is it safe?"

The OB laughed and said, "Yes. She will be just fine. It's not an uncommon procedure. Talk it over with your husband and then give the office a call. But don't wait too long. I'm on vacation starting January first."

After the workday, Jennifer wobbled into her house via the garage and dropped her bag onto the table near the back door. She was immediately greeted by her husband, Bryan, and their two-year-old, Taylor.

"Hi, babe," Bryan said, leaning down to give Jennifer a kiss before she landed squarely on a chair at their kitchen table while Taylor wiggled her way onto the shrinking, prime real estate that was Jennifer's lap. "How was work?"

Jennifer didn't want to talk about her day as a Customer Service Manager at a nearby Acme Supermarket, so she just blurted, "Dr. Potts wants to induce me right after Christmas."

Bryan chuckled and said, "Ka-ching. A second tax deduction for the tax year 2003."

Jennifer laughed genuinely, knowing that her CPA hubby loved a good tax break.

"Seriously, Bry. Are you okay with this? I don't know how I feel about this baby sharing a birthday month with her sister. But Dr. Potts said this little girl is going to be a whopper, and it's perfectly safe," she added in one single breath.

"I trust Dr. Potts. She was amazing when we had Taylor. But it's up to you, Mama."

Jennifer took a deep breath, which was the only breath she could manage these days, and said, "Let's do it."

So in the early evening of December 30, Jennifer was induced, and at 6:30 a.m. on December 31, Avery Marie Fellows came screaming into the world . . . almost as if she had a problem with the day she was born.

For the next several birthdays, to make things easier for family and friends during the Christmas month, Jennifer and Bryan set the first Sunday of December, which always fell close to Taylor's birthday of December 4, as the day to celebrate both girls. The guests were appreciative, as was Taylor, who delighted in having an audience to sing "Happy Birthday" to her.

DECEMBER 2008
Age 5

But at one particular December birthday party, Avery refused to stand next to Taylor in front of the cake. With some coaching/half carrying from her parents, Avery was reluctantly led to her spot. After Taylor's celebratory rendition of "Happy Birthday" was sung, everyone looked at Avery and began to sing, "Happy birthday, dear Avery. Happy birthday to you."

Avery just stood there.

Taylor nudged her sister, "It's your turn to blow out the candles."

Avery shook her head and folded her arms across her chest. Taylor nudged her sister again, and Avery shook her head again.

Taylor felt new-to-her emotions as her sister refused to participate. For the first time, Taylor was confused and a little sad. As she watched Avery, she couldn't decide if her little sister was angry or upset. Tears sprung to Taylor's eyes because, even at her young age of seven, she knew that she loved her sister. And she wanted Avery to be happy, too. Especially at their birthday party.

Before Taylor could start to full-on cry, her mom slid between her daughters and said, "On the count of three, we will all blow out Avery's candles. One . . . Two . . . Three."

Taylor and her mom did all the work because Avery plopped herself on the floor, arms still folded across her chest.

DECEMBER 2009
Age 6

The following year, Avery told her mom that she didn't want to share a birthday party with Taylor. She wanted to invite her school friends to a party at a local indoor kids' gym. Her mom agreed, but told Avery that it would have to be in the middle of January because their parents needed to recover from Christmas.

Avery had no idea what that meant and didn't like not being able to celebrate her birthday on her actual birthday. But Avery was happy that her friends would come and play with her, and they would not sing to her sister, too.

DECEMBER 2016-2020
Ages 13-17

As Avery grew, she became acutely aware that she'd been born on a day on which everyone celebrated. This fact made her feel disregarded, so when she was in eighth grade, she decided to experiment.

Avery and many of the kids from her class were invited to Katie D'Angelo's house for a New Year's Eve party, so Avery made sure to tell everyone who asked if she was going to Katie's party, "Yes. I'm going. And I'm excited that I will be with all my friends on my birthday." Or something to that effect.

New Year's Eve, or Avery's birthday as she called it, finally came, and Avery was anticipating a cake or something from Katie and her friends. But she was crushed when no one wished her a Happy Birthday or even mentioned it and, certainly, there was no cake.

Before she knew it, it was ten seconds to midnight, and she begrudgingly got caught up in the countdown to the New Year and blew on a party horn and yelled "Happy New Year!" with her friends. For Avery, though, the blowing of the party horn was emotionally indicative of the end of December 31 and a disappointing day rather than the introduction of a brand-new year.

Throughout high school, Avery developed a definitive love-hate relationship with New Year's Eve. She detested that it was her birthday but loved that she and her friends would gather at someone's house and drink whatever they could poach from their parents. Avery always grabbed a bottle of wine, which was in abundance at her house over the holidays. She became adept at using a wine opener during her sophomore year and briefly contemplated becoming a bartender after high school.

DECEMBER 2021-2023
Ages 18-20

When Avery started college, she told her roommates that her birthday was December 4, Taylor's birthday. She did this, she told herself, to alleviate any stressors to celebrate her on New Year's Eve, but in actuality, it was to keep her heart from being broken when no one appeared to care that it was her special day and not just a day to get drunk and kiss a random person when the New Year came dancing in at midnight.

Of course, Avery's close friends eventually learned that her birthday was on December 31, but they always wanted to celebrate with her at the beginning of December because they said that the end of the month was exceedingly challenging to get people together. After all, there are always a ton of holiday commitments, and so many of their friends went home between semesters. Naturally, Avery was annoyed by this. And disappointed in herself for never speaking up. And mad at her mother for being induced all those years ago. And still got upset when her dad called her "my little tax deduction."

Avery understood at her very core that her parents loved her so very much and found herself becoming more frustrated with herself as the invasive, negative feelings about the date inevitably permeated her brain. Perturbed by the nagging feeling that she was being ridiculous and immature, Avery gained some insight into the fact that she continually behaved like that little girl who crossed her arms and refused to blow out the candles.

DECEMBER 2024
Age 21

On her twenty-first birthday—December 31, 2024—Avery's best friends, Madison and Ava, decided to make a big deal about it. She was turning twenty-one, and this needed to be celebrated. Avery had helped plan both of their twenty-first parties, which were in perfect birthday months—March and June. These were months that people weren't super busy or broke.

The decision to have a birthday dinner party did not come easily for the two friends because Avery had always been prickly about her birthday. Madison had once said to Ava, "Avery is worse with her birthday than my Nana is. Nana stopped celebrating her birthday once she turned sixty." But Madison and Ava decided to invite all their friends to dinner to celebrate Avery's birthday anyway. This way, they could all head to a club to ring in the New Year afterward.

So, after finals were over in the second week of December, the friends called all the local places that could handle a large group but not one of the restaurants could accommodate them. After calling the fifth restaurant, Ava called Madison, who picked up on the first ring.

"I'm not having any luck with Avery's dinner. Were you able to get a reservation?" Ava asked hopefully.

"Not really. All of the usual places are booked. My dad suggested the Capital Grill, and I called the restaurant, and they said that they could accommodate us, but we would have to do a prix fixe menu, which starts at ninety dollars per person. Obviously, alcohol is extra."

Madison exhaled audibly, and Ava groaned on the other line. Both were well aware of their dire financial situations—they were all broke college students. Plus, the holidays were coming up.

Propelled by their love for Avery with her disdain for her birthdate, and their limited bank accounts, Ava and Madison three-way called Avery's older sister, Taylor, for advice.

Taylor immediately understood. She had been tiptoeing around Avery's birthday since her sister turned five and began to comprehend that her birthday was being hijacked every year.

Although she was momentarily pissed off at her sister's continued refusal to reframe the date as something more than an annual disappointment, she shook it off and came up with a solution.

"Okay, here's what we're going to do," Taylor began. "I'm going to take her out in the late afternoon for her first legal birthday drink. Then I'll bring her back to the apartment, and you'll have a surprise party waiting."

Both Ava and Madison audibly sighed in relief as they discussed details.

Madison, Ava, and Taylor made the choice to have food catered and delivered to the apartment that they shared with Avery. The e-vite read:

Shhh, It's a Surprise!
LET'S CELEBRATE AVERY FELLOWS' 21ST BIRTHDAY
December 31, 2024
7:00 p.m.
Dinner and Drinks
New Year's Celebration to Follow
Our Apartment
RSVP to Madison or Ava

The friends were apprehensive about including the New Year's part on the invitation because of Avery's vitriol surrounding New Year's Eve, but they were fearful that some people would leave early to go to another party. Or not show up at all because of other New Year's Eve plans. This way, everyone had a reason to come, stay, and celebrate their friend.

✦

On the day of the party, Avery spent the day with her sister, who kept her moving and not-very-lightly inebriated.

At 7:30 p.m., Taylor pulled into the parking garage of Avery's apartment complex. The sisters opted for the elevator to her third-floor apartment; Avery didn't think she'd make it up the stairs.

She staggered to her door and dug into her purse for her keys. Once she found them, she discovered that she couldn't get the key into the keyhole without leaning on the door. This was, of course, due to the single tequila shot she'd indulged in at each bar they went to.

After three attempts, Taylor took the keys from Avery and opened the door for her sister. As the door swung open, a chorus of "Happy Birthday!" pierced Avery's skull.

It took a minute for Avery to understand that there was a surprise party in her living room.

A surprise party. For her.

When the shock wore off, she allowed pure joy to overwhelm her. She happily hugged her sister and then cheerfully greeted Ava, Madison, and the other people who were gathered to celebrate her birthday . . . until she looked up at the *Happy 21st Birthday* banner only to see a *Happy New Year's* banner right below it.

Avery pushed her dislike for the 31st aside, walked to the alcohol setup, and poured herself a hearty glass of red wine. Taking a long sip of her drink, Avery envisioned herself being asleep by eleven-thirty and yet attempted to push all negative thoughts out of her head.

At that moment, there was a knock on the door.

Avery watched as Taylor opened the door for a very good-looking guy who said something to her sister. In turn, her sister pointed in the direction of Avery's friend Tyler. This new hottie walked over to Tyler, and they shook hands and did the man-hug thing. Tyler saw Avery looking their way and walked the hot guy over to her.

"Hey, birthday girl. This is my cousin, Liam. I hope it's okay that I asked him to come tonight," Tyler said sheepishly. Tyler's charisma helped him get away with pretty much anything.

Before Avery could answer, Liam quickly added, "I didn't know it was a birthday celebration. Happy birthday, Avery."

Avery held her breath for a usual follow-up comment such as "You're a New Year's baby" or "There's always a party on your birthday." But it didn't come.

Avery felt suddenly sober as she acknowledged her gratitude that this hot guy was not going to mention the fact that this day was anything more than her birthday.

"So, what have you done to celebrate this momentous occasion so far?" Liam asked earnestly.

Avery looked at Liam and, perhaps for the first time in twenty-one birthdays, smiled genuinely.

"We hit up every bar in the city," Avery said hyperbolically. "Apparently strangers love to buy drinks for people who are officially in the legal-aged club."

Liam chuckled.

Avery had to ask: "How did find yourself at my party?"

Liam told her that he was starting a new job in their city on January seventh and was getting settled in his new place. He jested, "Tyler felt sorry for me because he's the only person I know in this town."

Avery looked him square in the eyes and responded, "Now you know me."

Liam and Avery talked all that night and long into 2025. And then they talked year after year. Eventually, they married and decided to start a family.

DECEMBER 2030
Age 27

When Avery was told her due date, she was resolute. She knew what she would do if her child's birthday fell on a holiday. If necessary, she planned on transforming the date for her son and herself.

So, when Anders Fellows Daily was born on December 31, 2030, at 7:30 p.m., Avery knew exactly what to do. While Liam was sleeping on the roll-away bed, Avery picked up Anders from his newborn crib and brought him into the bed with her.

After setting him on her thighs, facing her, she whispered, "Happy birthday, my love. You will love having a birthday on this day. Everyone will wish you a happy birthday and wish you well for the upcoming year. You were born today because you are so very special and deserve all the people around the world to celebrate your day."

Avery paused and kissed the top of her son's head.

"You are a blessing and a gift."

From that day forward, New Year's Eve was Avery's favorite day of the year.

About the Author

Anna Picari is a storyteller and licensed therapist whose writing delves into complex dynamics of human relationships, personal growth, and healing. Drawing from her experience as a therapist, Anna crafts narratives that resonate with emotional authenticity and psychological depth. She is the author of *Lives Intertwined*, which released in 2024.

As a mother, spouse, and dog lover, Anna infuses warmth and relatability into her characters, often reflecting her own experiences with parenthood, relationships, and the everyday joys and struggles of life. Whether writing about a character's journey toward self-discovery or addressing mental health themes, Anna's open-minded and peaceful nature shines through.

When she's not writing or guiding clients through their healing journeys, Anna practices self-care through daily meditation, Peloton classes, and cooking Italian cuisine. She loves immersing herself in nature—whether hiking the scenic trails of Bucks County, Pennsylvania, or walking along the sandy shores of Fernandina Beach, Florida.

You can find Anna on:
Instagram @writtenbyannapicari

SEEKING SANCTUARY

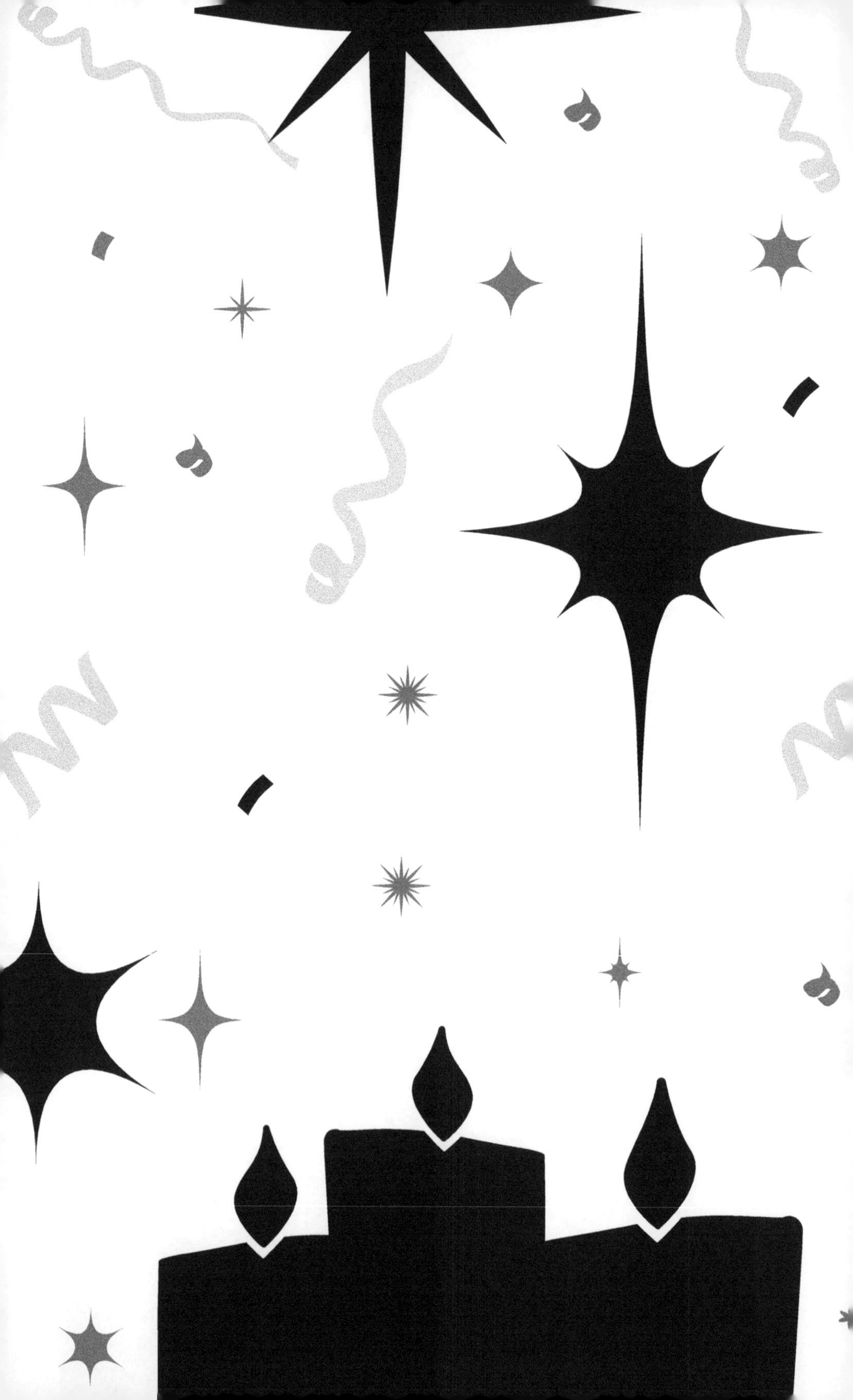

Seeking Sanctuary

Desi Stowe

I'M SITTING IN MY MAYBE temporary, but maybe permanent office, slowly spinning my chair like a bored eight-year-old who just had their video games taken away. My head is reclined as I methodically count ceiling tiles, trying to quell the ick feeling nestled in my stomach. Though I've entered the fourth decade of my life, I didn't seem to get both older and wiser. Just older. So I spin and count and try to figure out all the things. Eighteen, nineteen, twenty...

The knock on the door jars me out of my calm. Numbers calm me. I'm *that* person. Loads of fun at a party, let me tell ya. Invitations keep coming.

In walks the head of Human Resources, Vivian Ashmead, a leggy brunette who looks like she loves running more than she loves cake. I love running, too. But not more than cake. My first impression of her zeroed in on her intimidation factor. I've since learned it's more that she's a hard worker, dedicated, and doesn't take any nonsense from anyone about anything at any time. I love her and want to be her when I grow up. She's a good ten years my junior, but never mind that.

Her smile's warm and genuine, and she hands me a coffee. I have no doubt she can bust balls in a boardroom, but she's also thoughtful. Seriously, she's great. Goals.

"Priscilla, I'm so happy to see you!" She sits across from me and sips her coffee.

The coffee smells amazing, but I need more caffeine like I need a hole in my head. I'm already a jittery mess for this meeting. It feels like this moment is pivotal for my life. I'm not one for dramatics, ordinarily, but I need . . . something. I just need *something*.

I forgot I was supposed to respond to her. Lovely.

"Vivian, always a pleasure."

Did I just say that? Why do I sound so formal? Maybe I should crawl under my desk and hide my awkwardness there.

Vivian grins and gets straight to business. "You've been training under Eugene for a few weeks. It's time we determine the next steps. Do you want to stay in the Rehab Director position?"

This decision is what has me counting the tiles and feeling the ick. My insides are tied up in knots. I go with honesty because that's who I am. I never did learn the subtleties of white lies and gentle deception. Must have missed that day in school.

"Maybe?"

Instead of admonishing my indecision, Vivian leans back in the chair. Her pause makes me squirm, but only a little. "May I ask what's causing your hesitation?"

I press my lips together tightly, with enough force to make me aware of the expression. I take a deep breath, just like I teach my patients to do. I'm a physical therapist; breathing is an essential part of movement. Well, an essential part of anything except death.

I tap my brown-framed glasses. "I'm a nerd."

Vivian tilts her head, inviting me to offer more information beyond stating the obvious. This conversation seems to continue, regardless of whether I want it to or not. "I'm a nerd and I like numbers, research, and data. Things of that nature."

She smirks at me. "I know you do. I love that about you. We have that in common."

Vivian doesn't ask further questions. It's like she somehow knows I have a penchant for rambling. She'll get the information she wants if she gives me some time.

Besides, she's far from nerd territory. Why does this moment seem to matter so much to me? My job's important to me, and I make an effort to do good work. At the end of the day, though, it's just a job. It doesn't define me, it never has.

I've received workplace feedback before that I don't go above and beyond. And it's true. Bump my pay up well north of six figures, and we'll talk about above and beyond. Except today is different. Today the world is upside-down. Today is, well, weird. Lots of days in recent weeks have been weird.

I put my coffee down on the desk. "Can I level with you, Vivian?"

She gestures for me to continue. She somehow pulls off an intimidating presence and warm disposition simultaneously. I don't understand how she does it.

My eyes scan my space until I blankly stare at the fake plant in the corner of my office as if it holds some valuable truth. *It doesn't.*

"I'm not a people person. I get drained quickly. In hindsight, maybe a service-industry job where I'm surrounded by people wasn't the most brilliant of ideas."

This statement gets a chuckle from Vivian. "And?"

And everything is piling on me, and I feel like I'm drowning. My entire being is looking for rest and I don't know where to find it.

"Serving as director may give me a chance to use some of my love of data and research, allowing me to cater to my strengths."

Vivian scrunches her eyebrows together. "Isn't that a good thing?"

I hedge: "It is."

I grab my coffee again. Why do I keep doing that? It's like I need to keep its warmth near me, even if I don't drink it.

"But?" Vivian asks the question patiently. I'm sure she has a to-do list a mile long, but she's acting as though this conversation could last all day if I need it to.

"I'm just . . . it's just . . . I have to deal with people, too. Keep employees happy, do performance reviews, interview and hire. That sort of thing. People-y things. What if I can't do the people-y things?"

Let's be real here, people-y things are my downfall. Always have been.

Vivian leans forward, eyes locked on mine. "You've worked in the trauma unit. I know from Eugene how difficult that can be. Performance reviews and other management tasks will be a walk in the park for you. Plus, I've got your back. I want you to succeed."

Vivian and Eugene, my former boss, hooked up at some point recently. Eugene decided to open his own practice, only recently leaving the hellish world of hospital hallways in search of something better. I hope he finds it, and I don't begrudge him for trying. Burnout spreads quicker around here than head lice at a daycare center. Both are annoying and invasive.

"I want to succeed. I, uh . . . I *need* to succeed."

Vivan searches my face. "Why is success so important to you?

I'm all for success, don't get me wrong. But I'm getting the impression there's more at play here."

Yeah. There's more at play. An understatement for sure.

A recently failed marriage, for one. A betrayal by an ex-husband who left me because I chose to fund our mortgage over his lavish lifestyle and love for designer clothes. Seriously. You can't make up the things that happen in my life. He's already married again, before the ink was even dry on our divorce papers. I hope they're absolutely miserable. If you're looking for someone willing to be the better person, that person would not be me.

"My personal life's a train wreck."

I absently run my thumb around my bare ring finger. It's been naked for weeks now, but somehow I keep looking for it.

Vivian gets it. I can tell by the look on her face. "You need your professional life to go well to make up for your struggles in your personal life? Am I understanding correctly?"

"Bingo. I don't want this promotion if I'm not going to be successful. I'm not in the right head-space to handle another failure."

I set down my coffee again. This back-and-forth with the coffee is ridiculous, but I can't seem to stop it.

Vivian looks at me for a long time as if she's sizing me up and figuring me out. She breaks the silence with an offer. "You'll be fine, professionally. I'll take you under my wing and personally be your mentor if you want that. But Priscilla, I've been in those shoes. Throwing everything into work doesn't take away from the personal struggles. You can't run from them forever. Believe me, I tried."

I know some of this story from talking with Eugene. Despite Vivian putting her all into her career, some undeserving dude got the promotion. Misogyny 101, lesson one: bypass the woman who's been doing the work. I hate it for her. No one deserves that kind of treatment. I hope Vivian's former boss is miserable, too.

"I realize I can't run from my struggles forever, but I do want a distraction. I want to take the director position. If you have the time and energy to help me and can take on the role of mentor, I can do it. Even the people-y parts."

Vivian laughs and shakes my hand before coming around my desk to forego formality and hug me. "I'm excited about this!"

I give her a squeeze. Maybe I'm a teeny bit excited, too.

Vivian then slides a square box out from beneath the small stack of notepads and tablet she's been balancing on her lap. She places it on my empty desk in front of me. It's a day-to-day tear-away desk calendar of happy hedgehogs.

"Eugene told me you like hedgehogs. I thought it'd be both a fun and a practical gift. Only a few days until you get to start it!"

I clutch the calendar to my chest and squeal. "I love hedgehogs!"

Smiling, I pull out my keys from my desk drawer. Clipped to my keyring is a small hedgehog plush my niece gave me for Christmas.

Vivian takes my keys from me, laughing. She inspects the plush and nods her approval. "Then the desk calendar suits you?"

"It does, I love it. Thank you. It's a kind gesture." Vivian has made my day with her offer of mentorship and the thoughtful gift.

She stands up to leave. "New year, new job?"

I nod. "New year, new job." Silently, I add, *and new me.*

Alone again in my office, I spin my chair. This time it's with a bit more enthusiasm. Instead of counting tiles, I look around the small room. Now that it's mine, I should decorate it with my style. What is my style? I'm not sure.

Three months ago, I left the attorney's office after a bitter battle. My ex-husband fought, fought hard I might add, for me to pay alimony *and* half his student loans. My attorney laughed in his face, and we agreed only to split assets fifty-fifty and go our separate ways. The Ex's last words to me were: "You were always useless."

Well, I disagree. Useless isn't my style. I'm just not sure what my style is.

The battle cut deep and scarred me. I'd loved this man at some point. In the depths of my soul, I knew I wasn't *useless*. At forty-two, I've been given the unexpected gift of a clean slate. I just have no idea what to do with it, other than agree to this promotion. Distraction and rogue thoughts prevent me from working anyway, so I answer the call from my mom lighting up my phone screen.

"Hello, dear! I just wanted you to know I emailed you several articles about how to get your man back." Her voice is chipper for someone who's being so unreasonable and obnoxious. Besides, I already saw the articles and deleted them.

I sigh. This is a road well-traveled.

"Mom, he's gone. Married to someone else. Living the dream. Don't worry about me, though. I'm going to adopt seven cats after work today. It's time I committed to my Cat Lady persona." I say this as a joke but consider its merits. Maybe that's who I am and I should own it. *Cat Lady just might be my style! Wait. Is Hedgehog Lady a thing?*

My mother, never one to let things go, continues, "That girl's just a rebound. Your sister thinks that his sham of a second marriage is already falling apart. The commitment the two of you made is for life. Your father and I have been married for forty-four years now. You can't just quit being married. It takes work."

"Yeah, staying married was the plan." I didn't ask to enter my forties as a recent divorcée.

"Priscilla, dear, your husband brought out a playful side to you. He was good for you. You're typically so withdrawn, and he pushed you out of your shell." Her voice wanders into an almost reasonable tone.

She's not entirely wrong. He's charismatic and charming. People assumed I was, too, if only by association. My issue was more his reckless disregard for our bank balance. He didn't want to live with any financial constraints. I wanted to be able to eat and pay my bills. I finally respond. "The marriage was at an impasse. It couldn't last, it couldn't go on. Besides, he's moved on. It's time I did, too."

"You remember your Aunt Mia." It's a statement and not a question.

"Of course, I do." Every part of me wants to avoid the topic of Mom's sister. The only other divorcée in our otherwise picture-perfect family.

"She was never happy after her divorce." She says this as if it's the final say on divorce. If one person wasn't happy, then there's no way I could be. Maybe she's right, and I won't be happy. But I wasn't happy in marriage, either.

"Look, Mom. I know this isn't what you wanted. It's not what I wanted either."

"Then, change it! Win him back!" Her voice raises over the call, and I hold the phone away from my ear.

Because I have nothing else to say about this, because I need my mom to let it go, because I cannot have this conversation, yet again, I start singing the theme song from the movie *Frozen*. She finds this zero percent funny, which is inaccurate. It's at least forty percent funny.

Bitter frustration laces my mom's words. "You want him back." It's not posed as a question.

That's just the thing. I don't. I don't want him back. For the first time ever, I admit as much to my mom and myself. I'm currently broke and without friends because he took every last thing from me. A long list of expletives that would rival that of a sailor comes through my phone.

I take a deep breath in hopes of finding calm. "Mom, please listen. I don't want him back. My life is better without him in it."

Her answer is some incoherent grumbling followed by, "You've always been so selfish. He's part of our family! You can't just ditch him."

I'm done with this conversation to nowhere. "He ditched me. He moved on. You should, too." I know my mom loved the Ex. He bought her expensive gifts and flowers. Doted on her to no end. With my money. Mom hangs up angry at me and I am, once again, alone.

It's lunchtime, but my unappealing leftovers stare back at me without offering temptation. I can eat those tomorrow; it's time to celebrate my wins in life. I'm officially a director and have an office.

I opt to have lunch at this little place next door, Checklist Chicken. They have a chicken sandwich made of sin, salt, and a zillion calories. *It's time to feed my feelings.*

The smell of grease and goodness nearly knocks me down. Everything is right with the world. It's odd that I'm here. I'm almost a vegetarian. Some might say I'm terrible at it, but I'd disagree. The only exceptions to my plant-based diet are a Checklist Chicken sandwich and Canadian bacon on my Hawaiian pizza. I've never been an all-or-nothing kind of gal anyway.

Walking past the decorated trees and lights, I make my way

through the restaurant. I'm bah-humbug about the holiday season this year, but even I can admit the decor is a nice touch. The back booth is secluded and calls to me. The grease from the sandwich moisturizes my cuticles and clogs my arteries. It's amazing. If I consume enough greasy food, will it give me the strength I need to manage my team? Can I do this? Will my mom forgive me for my failed marriage? Is Hedgehog Lady my style? What do I want?

The questions all remain unanswered.

I return to my office, which is weird enough. I've always worked roaming around the hospital and logging into random computers when I needed it. I've never had an office space that was just mine.

If I'm going to be a director, I should probably work. However, my day is interrupted again, this time by Eugene Spinner, who's easy on the eyes and also isn't annoying. It's hard to find both in the same person.

My former director smiles my way. "I met Vivian for lunch and thought I'd stop by to congratulate you. You're going to do great as the new director."

I brush back my rather unruly, wavy hair and raise my eyebrows, but I don't deflect the compliment. This job *is* the perfect fit for me right now. Maybe.

Either way, I'm hoping the change in responsibilities pulls me out of the stupid funk I've been lodged in now for months. Maybe years, if anyone's keeping score.

"Sure. I got this."

"I know you do." Eugene chuckles and sits across from me. He'd already helped train me on my responsibilities before he left. In a nutshell, I'm here to advocate for the rehab team's needs, attend meetings with hospital administration, and deal with complaints and employee issues.

I'd been dealing with my coworkers and their nonsense long before I took this position. I find myself counseling them on various work and personal needs. Somehow me being one of the older physical therapists here means that I'm also supposed to be the wisest.

Yeah, right.

I shrug at the man sitting across from me. "I think I need something new. This should help."

Eugene gives me a lopsided grin. "I understand that feeling." We chat amiably about employees that may cause problems and day-to-day to-do lists, and he answers all my remaining questions with a professionalism that is, quite frankly, rare for someone so young. I sigh. I like Eugene and didn't want to see him go. We'd worked together for a few years.

He hugs me goodbye and then walks away from me. From management. From hospital work. Hopefully toward something that makes him smile. An unanswered question forms in my mind: What makes *me* smile?

The workday lingers, and I try to wrap my brain around my new responsibilities before leaving and meeting my sister, Sheila, for our monthly dinner date. Sheila inherited all the poise and confidence of our shared genetic pool, leaving me with a love for numbers and depression. Even so, I love my nature-fearing sister. But she's a handful.

I tell her of my new job—a promotion, the only one of my career. I'd been excited to share my success with her tonight. Unfortunately, she seems to have left her poise at home.

"Priscilla, that's a monumentally bad idea."

Her words shock me, and I just stare at her, waiting for an explanation. In hindsight, I should've walked away then.

She continues, "First of all, no one ever listens to you."

No one in our family listens to me, that's true. Even my wedding catered to the whims and wishes of others. Professionally, I've formed more balanced relationships, and I interrupt her to say as much.

She waves me off, dismissing my words and unintentionally proving my point. "No one listens to you."

Why does this hurtful phrase require repetition?

"I love you, truly I do, but you couldn't hold a marriage together. Why do you think you can keep a team of employees together?"

She's in full-out rant mode, so I can't sneak in a word.

"Your hair needs some work, and when was the last time you had a manicure? You've got so much you need to be working on. The last thing you need to do is take on responsibilities that you can't handle. You can't even handle your own life!"

My eyes burn with hurt and unshed tears from the verbal slap in the face my sister just gave me. Sure, I've had all the thoughts she's just voiced run through *my* head over the past few days, but for her to flippantly articulate my deep-rooted fears hurts.

I glare at her. "That was uncalled for."

It's the closest I can come—that I've ever come—to standing up for myself.

She rolls her eyes. "It's the truth and you know it. You can back out of the position tomorrow. Look, we have more important things to discuss. You know Mom's rented the clubhouse again for New Year's Eve."

Inwardly, I groan. Our Christmas celebrations are typically very small and low-key. Then, my family puts on this huge New

Year's Eve celebration every year. It's so people-y and filled with fake niceties. I hate every second of it.

My chest starts to feel tight. I can't do it this year. I can't smile politely while people send me fake pity and concern about my divorce. In my mind, I start feigning an illness that will happen precisely on the last day of December.

"Don't start thinking of excuses. You're coming." My sister interrupts my thoughts with her harsh words. Why is she so angry with me?

Groaning, I place my head in my hands. My very soul is longing for quiet.

"I don't know if I can handle it this year."

Her eyes lock on mine. "You want to come. It's what we've always done."

"What if what I've always done is no longer working for me? And what is your deal today?"

Venom laces her words and anger fills her eyes. "You don't see how hurtful this is! My daughters deserve to have an uncle, and you stole that away from them!"

Her rant catches me by surprise, as have most of what she's said to me today, and I'm rendered speechless. The Ex was a horrible uncle anyway, somehow thinking that children were beneath him and not worth his time. He did buy them nice presents, though, with the money I earned, of course. Somehow, he got the credit for that, too.

She's on a roll and not finished with her tirade. "Now you're saying you don't want to go to our New Year's Eve Party?! We've already rented the clubhouse!"

"Over a hundred people will be there. No one will miss me." What they will miss is me handling the majority of the cleanup, but I don't say that.

My mind drifts back to my sweet niece. "Is my being an aunt not enough for your girls? The Ex left me. He's gone. Remarried. What am I supposed to do about it?"

I shove my food away as nausea creeps its way into my body.

My sister softens her prickly exterior, but only slightly. "Are you still not on any kind of social media? He's divorced again. Separated, at least."

Divorced again? Already? Is that some kind of record for the shortest marriage, ever?

Social media is something I avoid. My sister knows this but has been pestering me to plaster my face and my life across the World Wide Web. No thanks. "You know I'm not."

"Ugh, you're such a grandma! Could you please live in this century? Mom invited him on New Year's Eve. Listen to me, please. It's your chance to right some wrongs. To fix what's broken. New Year's Eve is your only shot at redemption." Her voice is pleading, as if it's trying to find some reasonable ground after hurling insults at me.

Redemption? Really? I close my eyes and try to picture what I want in my life, and it's hard to see a clear picture. That's exactly why I took this new job as a reset.

Wordlessly, I stand up and ignore the glare coming from my sister. I throw cash on the table to cover my uneaten dinner.

She takes a deep breath. "Priscilla, I just want what's best for you. We all do." That's a sentiment that's hard to believe after the verbal assault I've just received. I shake my head. "You don't know what's best for me."

"Do you?"

Her question hangs in the air between us, unanswered as I head to the parking lot. Surely, my evening can't get worse, but then it does.

There he is.

Tall, artificially blonde, and irritating.

The Ex, casually leaning against my car. Dressed in designer clothes he can't afford and looking exactly like my biggest regret.

"Move." My single-word greeting doesn't seem to rattle him.

"No. We need to talk." He folds his arms across his chest, and I search my heart to figure out why I used to love this man. Despite my every wish not to have this conversation, he continues, "Your mom has offered to pay me a rather lavish sum of money if we remarry. She called it a 'second wedding gift.'"

Bile burns my throat, and I want to deny the truth of this betrayal. Except I know that it's probably true. My mom loves him, probably more than she loves me. She never saw that his lavish gifts and ridiculous level of charm was all showmanship. Not that I fault her for it; he's an amazing actor. She basked in the attention he gave her.

I pull out my phone and call my mom. I ask her, then and there, with The Ex standing by. She doesn't deny it.

The smug expression on his face makes me sick to my stomach. I push him out of the way so I can get to the car door when he spins me around and pins me between his body and the car door.

"Priscilla, I need this money. Your family wants this. Why fight it? It's not like you've got a long line of men ready to take my place. It wouldn't matter if you did. You want me."

Through gritted teeth, I say, "Get. Off. Me."

He doesn't budge, so I knee him in the groin. Hard.

As he's groaning in pain, I push him away, he trips over a curb, and falls onto the gravel surface of the parking lot, moaning in the fetal position.

My sister runs out of the restaurant and has the unforgivable audacity to check on him. I get in my car and speed away.

The next day, I head to work wearing more than my simple make-up routine as I try to hide the remnants of the tears of betrayal I cried the night before. Is my mother so ashamed of *my* divorce that she'd pay someone to *take* me? Why can't I just be alone? Am I not enough on my own? Everything feels so exhausting.

Vivian comes into my office as scheduled. I admit I'm not sure I can do this job and am considering backing out of the offer. My sister's words burn deep into my memory where they cause all my repressed self-doubt to surface.

"I understand the hesitation. If you don't want this job then I shred the paperwork and start my search from scratch. It's not a matter of your inability, though." She meets my gaze and holds it for a beat before asking me the question I need to hear. "What do *you* want?"

My modus operandi is stoicism. I forgot to bring it to work today and collapse back in my chair, running my hands over my face to stifle the groan of defeat that escapes.

Vivian sits down during my dramatics. Nonchalantly, she pulls out a legal pad and a pen. When curiosity causes me to look up, she again asks, "What is it that *you* want?"

I shake my head no.

"Look, I do feel like I'm coming apart at the seams here, but it's not a work problem."

Pausing my words, I remember my sister's doubts about my ability to succeed as a director.

"It's not *only* a work problem, anyway. Typically, I can compartmentalize my work and my personal life. I admit that's a struggle today."

Grabbing a pen, Vivian writes down the words *What do you want?* on the legal pad.

Am I in a counseling session? It feels like it. She takes a moment, presumably to gather her thoughts.

"Despite our best efforts, at times our work affects our personal lives, and vice versa. I'd like to think we're friends. If you want to tell me what's going on, I'm happy to listen."

Are we friends?

I close my eyes and weigh the idea of inviting Vivian into my dumpster fire life. She offers me a peaceful silence that breaks down my defenses.

"Last night I had dinner with my sister. She not-so-helpfully decided to point out that I can't handle my personal life so how could I possibly handle this job?"

I go on to tell her the short version of my awful divorce, of The Ex divorcing his second wife and my mom offering him—not me, not us—a large sum of money to reconcile with me. Then, for good measure, I tell her of my altercation with him in the parking lot where I left him rolling on the ground in pain.

She dissolves into a full-out laugh, doubled over and tears escaping her eyes. "Priscilla!! You, my friend, are my hero."

"You've got a pretty flexible definition of hero," I deadpan.

This statement makes her laugh even more. Then she taps on her legal pad. "You've told me what your sister wants. What your mom wants. What your ex wants. What do *you* want?"

In a voice barely above a whisper, I say, "I want to see the Golden Gate Bridge."

I spent fifteen years in a marriage with a man who hated traveling, only because it took away from his desperate, yet failed, attempts at becoming wealthy. I don't know how he planned to achieve upper-class status by selling cars. It always seemed like a pipe dream to me. But I love to travel, and I've spent years neglecting my own desires.

"How's the department holiday coverage?" She writes down *Golden Gate Bridge* on her notepad.

"We are pretty limited on coverage until tomorrow, the twenty-eighth, then it gets better."

I pull up my staffing calendar to verify the date.

"I traveled a lot in my last job. I have more frequent flier miles than I'll ever use." Vivian's fingers move deftly over her phone. "For clarification purposes, I'm gifting you a flight as a friend and not as a fellow employee or as Human Resources Director."

"I'm sorry, what?"

Did she just say what I think she said?

My email pings with approval for personal time off from December 29 until January 2.

"That was scary fast. How do you even work that fast?"

She gives me a puzzled look. "What?"

My voice raises slightly, more animated than my norm. "What do you mean, 'what'? You just approved time off that I didn't ask for and said you'd handle my flight!"

My emotions oscillate between exasperation and excitement. Could I really go to San Francisco for New Year's Eve? Shirk my so-called responsibilities and do something for myself? My head spins with options and possibilities.

She leans across the desk and grabs my arm. "Oh, I'm so sorry. I just railroaded you like your family's been doing."

She releases my arm to hide her face behind her hands and apologizes again.

"I'm goal oriented. I can get carried away. I'm so, so sorry."

My voice softens and my heart warms. "You may have railroaded me a bit, but it was because you wanted to help me out. It came from a good place. If someone is trying to railroad me into happiness, who am I to complain?"

She circles the desk and hugs me. "If you want to go to San Francisco for New Year's Eve, then go. Do it for you. Maybe your family will learn to appreciate you in your absence. Maybe you can check off a bucket-list item. Maybe you can find perspective in the misty fog surrounding the Golden Gate Bridge. It's a beautiful area, well worth the visit. If you want my help, I can help you." She pauses before adding, "I *want* to help you."

My look borders on suspicion, I'm sure, and my words escape at a slow, even tempo. "Why do you want to help me?"

"Because before coming here, I'd spent my career railroading people—not toward happiness, mind you. I could use a bit of atonement. And also, because we're friends? Right?" She gives me a soft smile.

My style isn't self-care or friendship. Even so, I said I needed something new, didn't I?

I accept Vivian's friendship and her help securing a flight and a nice place to stay. My lack of travel experience would've made finding last minute travel and accommodations a daunting task. Vivian helps me do this at lightning speed.

I've ignored my phone all day. But after work, I see about a zillion messages. Confirmation that my family has invited The Ex to our New Year's Eve celebration. My sister admonishing me for assaulting The Ex in the parking lot. I guess him pinning me against my car falls in the realm of acceptable behavior. I sit in my kitchen with my laptop and compose three separate emails. My entire being is longing for some respite from the nonsense. In order to find it, I'm going to have to establish some boundaries. I *want* boundaries.

The first email is to my mom acknowledging her hurt from my divorce. It did hurt her; he was her son-in-law for fifteen years. However, I made it clear that I was not attending her New Year's Eve party this year, nor any other function where he was invited.

As for her selling me off? Paying The Ex to remarry me? Yeah, that's too much to deal with right now. That's an in-person conversation for the New Year. While I'm the one who experienced divorce, my family is acting out in a spectacularly dramatic fashion. The reason isn't entirely known to me, but what I do know is I can't be a part of their fallout when I'm dealing with my own.

The second email is to my sister. I let her know her words hurt me and let her know not to contact me until after the New Year. Space and time will hopefully ease the pain of our last dinner, although I'm not sure. Especially after she sided with The Ex in the parking lot.

Forgiveness is a hard pill to swallow. Frankly, I'm not sure that it's deserved, but she's my sister. What is life without the dysfunctional love of a sibling?

The last email is to The Ex. The email sets the firm boundary that says if he ever is in my physical space again, I'll get a restraining order. He's even older than I am, and it's not my fault he's struggling financially. Those struggles are of his own doing and are his own problem.

With needed correspondence checked off my to-do list, the next item is to pack. In a robotic and methodical fashion, I fold clothes to take on my trip. An undercurrent of worry seeps into my being at the response I'll receive. Boundaries have been set for maybe the first time in my life. *EVER*. It creates a heady mixture of apprehension and freedom.

On New Year's Eve, I dress in black dress pants, a simple pair of boots, and a deep blue cashmere sweater. I splurged for a new gray pinstripe winter coat for this trip. *Not too bad*, I think as I look into the mirror.

I make my way to the water's edge and step onto a boat. The hotel concierge helped me secure the required ticket for a midnight cruise of the San Francisco Bay. He shot me a sympathetic glance when I asked if he could secure a single ticket, but I've never been happier. Not in recent years, anyway. Tonight doesn't require a plus-one.

Happiness doesn't require a plus-one.

The boat drifts away from the shore and into the gentle waters of the bay. Symbolic of leaving the ick of this less-than-fabulous year behind. The noise around me is boisterous and energetic, a fitting atmosphere for the evening.

Gradually, I move through the crowd and find a quieter place where I can perch on the boat railing. I consider how the future seems unavoidable on the last day of December. As I think of the year ahead, I'm filled with mostly trepidation. It's too overwhelming to think of resolutions or goals for the entire year. Despite the strong sense of fear, hope leaks into the crevices of my mind. It's a welcomed companion even if it's a faint whisper and not something that's fully formed.

Instead of the daunting routine of New Year's resolutions, I opt for a monthly goal. Maybe I can take this next year in small, bite-sized pieces. Officially beginning my new job is a great start. In February, I'll decide on my next goal. An idea is already forming in my mind: nurturing friendships.

I've spent the past few years putting my all into saving my failing, dumpster fire of a marriage. My support bubble, a natural consequence of my neglect, dissolved, leaving me alone. I pull out my phone and send a text to Vivian, telling her thank you and Happy New Year. Then I stow my device away. I don't need it anymore tonight.

The Golden Gate Bridge lights up in the colorful explosion of fireworks as "Auld Lang Syne" plays in the background. The troubles and turmoil of recent years slowly slide away, falling into the deep waters around me. No doubt those troubles will return in full force once I'm home. But for now, I know what I want. Maybe, even just for tonight, I'm seeking sanctuary. As cheers erupt around me at the stroke of midnight, I think I've found it.

"Seeking Sanctuary" is a standalone short story that exists in the Charleston Harbor Series by Desi Stowe. The events in "Seeking Sanctuary" occur simultaneously with the ending of **Shadows.** *The Charleston Harbor Series can be found on Kindle Unlimited, Amazon ebook, and via paperback at most major retailers and independent bookstores.*

About the Author

While Desi Stowe officially started writing in early 2022, she'd been developing her scaffolding as a writer for many years. She'd answer requests of "hey, can you word this better for me?" and the like. She had a way with words and a love of stories. Writing was a natural next step. She also found that writing was a wonderful escape into a fictional world, even if that world mirrored real life. She worked to combine her experience in healthcare and her love of writing into her first novel. In February of 2024, she published *Done*, her first novel of the Charleston Harbor Series. Only a few months later, she was able to publish a sophomore novel, *Shadows*. She lives in Raleigh, North Carolina, with her husband and two children. During the day, she works as a physical therapist. Her writing has been in sporadic spurts while juggling other responsibilities. Desi often finds herself daydreaming about plot progression and character arcs while working out or washing dishes. The characters of her novels have a special place in her heart and hopefully yours, as well.

You can find Desi on:
Instagram @desistowe

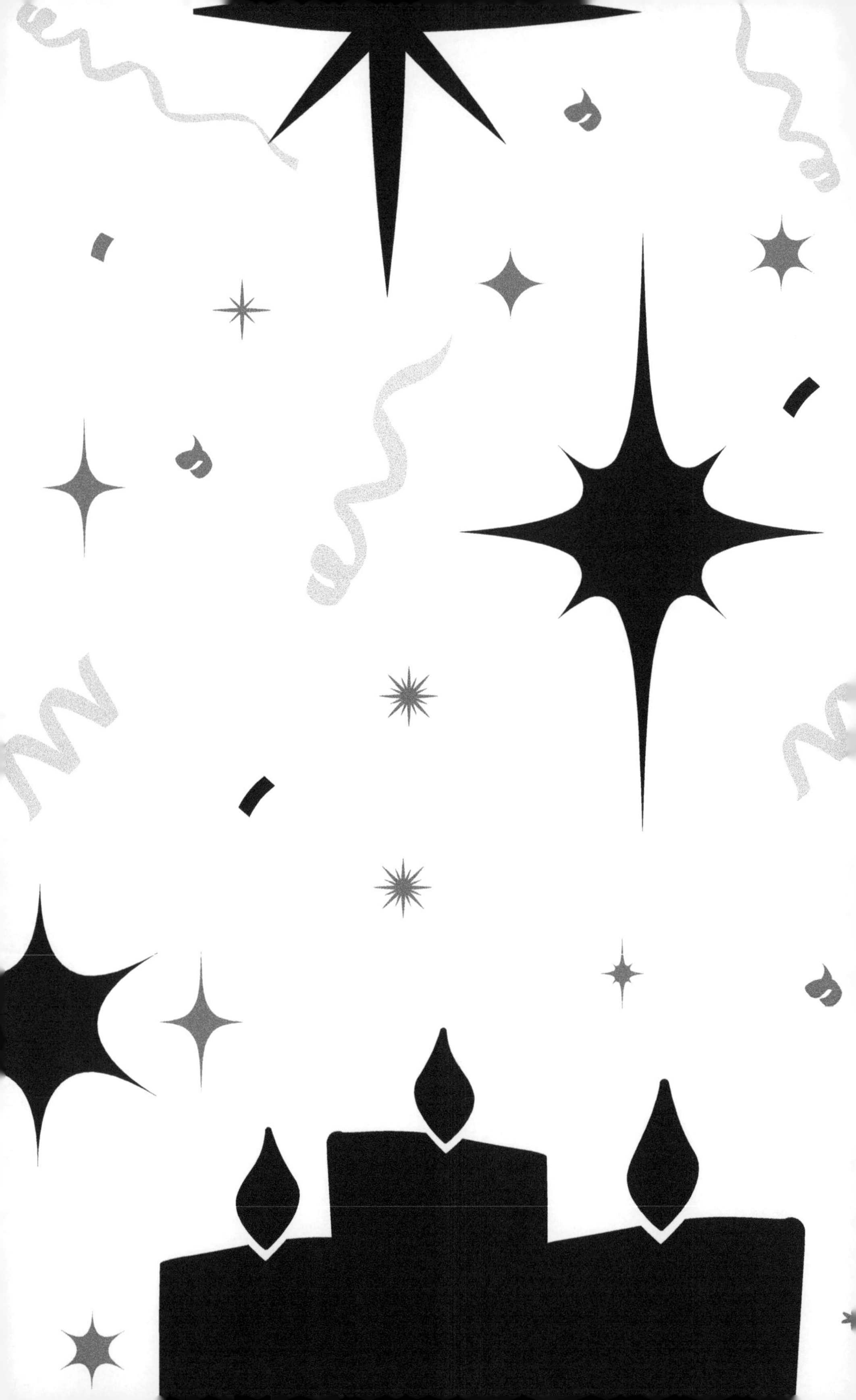

POLKA DOTS

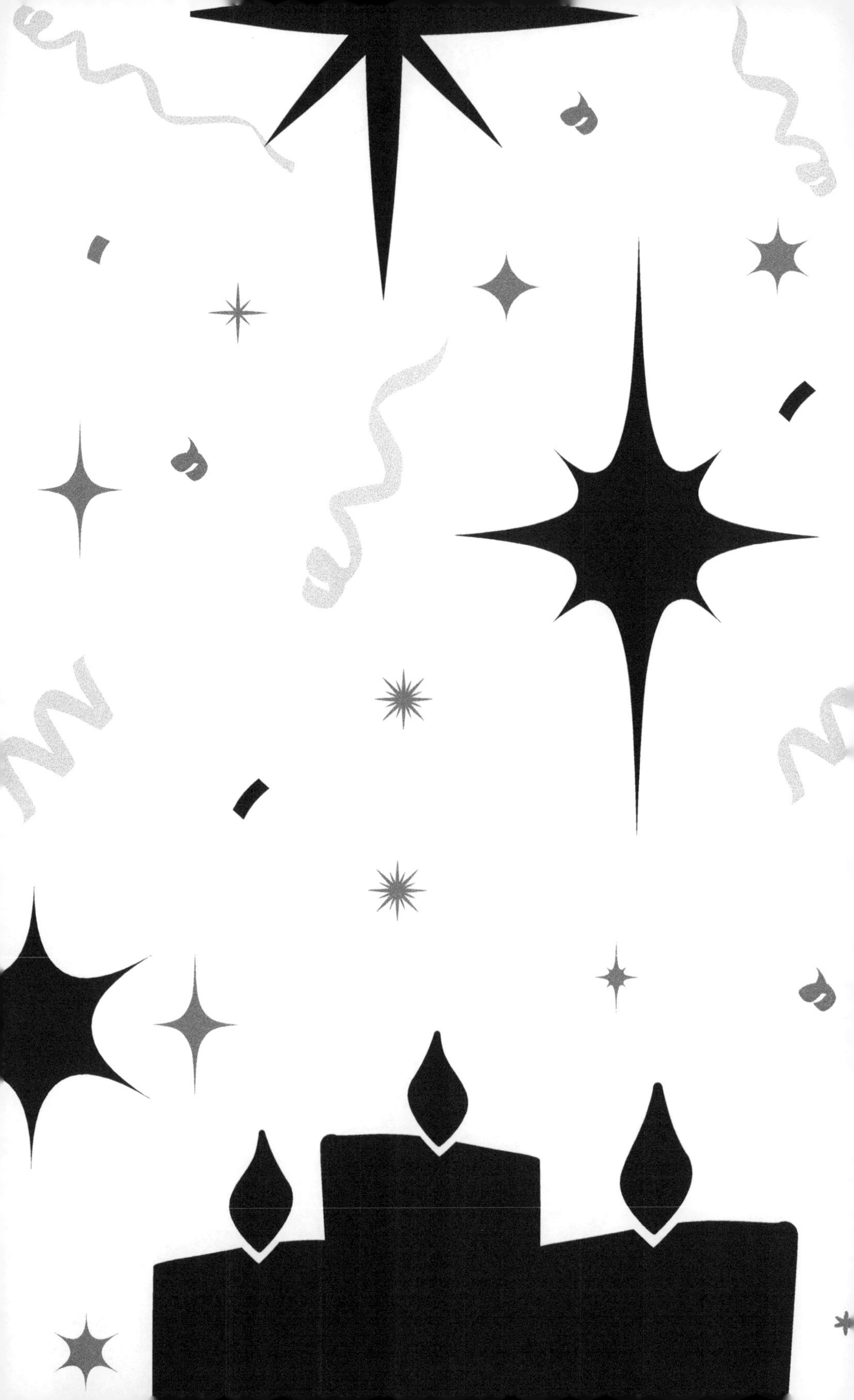

Polka Dots

Mitch S. Elrick

"TWO-DOLLAR PINTS DON'T DRINK themselves! Let's go out!"

My roommate is one of those people who doesn't invite you to do something. He tells you to do it.

Without raising my eyes from my book, I say, "No, I'm reading." Which is sort of true. Really, I was thinking about purple and pink polka dots, but it looked like I was reading, so I stick with that.

"Come on!" He nudges me. "We always have fun at The River."

"No." I pretend to be final.

But, really, it's just a knee-jerk response; this dance has been danced before.

And it's not that I don't want to go out. Of course I do. We always have a good time. But being financially independent as a sophomore in college doesn't exactly leave a lot of room for "play" money. And even if I did have enough to go out, which I do, that isn't the only issue.

Lately, my jeans have started transitioning to jeggings and my T-shirts show off my belly button when I sit on couches. One could have described my Freshman Fifteen more accurately as a Sophomore Twenty-Four. And I'm a junior now, so . . . You can imagine that math and the cutesy rhyme to go along with it.

I had been slender in high school, but since beer, wings, and dollar menus are the Father, Son, and Holy Spirit of college life, I have become a patron saint.

Forgive me Father for I have binged.

All around, it's been time for a change, and what better time than the new year just a couple weeks away?

But that's the thing about roommates who double as best friends. They couldn't care less about the "New Year, New Me" mantra.

"Come on!" he presses. "Think about it: when you get your teaching license and get a job, you're going to be grading and doing lesson plans and all that other shit our teachers did back when we were in school. And you know what they were thinking when they had us in class?"

"No."

But I must say, I do appreciate his confidence in me finding a job after graduation.

Henry takes in a deep breath as he heaves, "I WISH I WOULD HAVE GOTTEN HAMMERED WHEN I HAD THE CHANCE! Now I have to deal with these ugly, smelly kids all day and grade their stupid, shitty papers all night!"

My eyes don't leave the page. If they do, he'll know he's got me.

"I'm not ugly or smelly. That *was* and *still is* you."

Ignoring my jab completely, he stomps his foot like a two-year-old who didn't get the cereal they wanted in the grocery store aisle.

"Going to bed sober on Modelo Monday is illegal—punishable by law! How do you expect to get a teaching license with a criminal record? I don't want to have to turn you in, but I am a respected citizen of this community, and I will do what I must for my country."

My eyes roll so hard I see brain cells die. "Besides," he adds, "my treat. Dinner, too."

Unfortunately, financial desperation breeds stupidity, especially for twenty-year-olds. And I am no exception.

I look up, annoyed. "Okay, but only one tonight. I have class tomorrow."

I'm only going to be five-ish minutes late, which isn't bad because I'm usually ten-ish minutes late. Stale beer breath and a heavy pounding in my head make the walk to my 8:00 a.m. class a real joy. About halfway through my stroll, the sun decides to show its face, which is awesome, because if there's anything I love more than walking through a foot of snow while producing throw-up burps every three steps, it's getting to do all that while the sun bullies my retinas.

With soggy feet and a can't-do attitude, I open the door to the lecture hall and it croaks extra loud, snitching on me.

The annoyed professor jaws as she sips her coffee. I find a seat near the back, trying to be as invisible as possible. As I sink into the chair, I fold the desk over, and as it comes down, it makes contact with my gut, which is the perfect amount of salt to this morning's hangover wound. Before taking out my laptop, I silently vow to do a couple extra miles on the treadmill.

The professor drones on while the rest of us tip-tap at our machines, and my focus begins to drift, as it often does in this class, to the upper-left corner of the room. But it's not my fault. It's the polka dots.

Dark purple. Hot pink outlining. White background.

There are many JanSport backpacks with this design, especially in the education department, but these aren't just any polka dots. Couldn't forget them if I tried. Perhaps that's because I couldn't care less about the backpack, or the polka dots, but that I more so fancied its owner.

We've never talked before, there hasn't really been an opportunity. I guess I could have created one. I've done it before. But this was different. I couldn't just go in with some bullshit line. I had to be strategic. That's what I told myself at the beginning of the semester. But that was warm-and-sunny August, full of hope and promise, when all I had to do was set my fantasy football lineup and stare at the cute girl in my eight o'clock class. Now it's freeze-your-ass-off December, our last week of class, nonetheless. And don't you dare ask about my fantasy team. I can't control injuries.

I'll probably see her on campus, but it's unlikely I'll have any classes with her next semester. We start field work so most of our "class work" will be online.

Being one of maybe five males surrounded by countless females in all of my classes may seem like this cis male's dream, but one wrong move and all of a sudden you're the creep of the cohort. Can't have that.

Which is why I'm *such a big fan* of dark purple and hot pink polka dots. Always have been. Backpack designs are SO awesome! I care about them so much!

It's not pathetic. I've convinced myself of that. Maybe a little weird. Okay, weird at the very least.

My headache is getting worse. I need a burrito.

For some inexplicable reason, the intermixing of cig smoke and an oily garage is somewhat comforting. And so is the Budweiser swivel stool I'm sitting on. There's a rip in the upholstery that my fingers make worse every time I sit. But it's fine, the padding is still intact. Mostly.

"So why didn't you just talk to her after class?"

Smoke clouds above Henry as he tinkers inside the hood of his '67 Chevelle. I don't know shit about cars so don't expect me to elaborate. It's a car. It was a piece of shit when he bought it. And, over time, the shittiness has greatly dissipated. I'd never say this to his face, but it's wildly impressive—like it's one of those cars you see fancy gangsters driving in the Scorsese movies. So, it's baffling how someone with so much raw intelligence can seem to muster up such stupid questions.

Why didn't I just talk to her after class? Oh, yeah, Henry, why didn't I think of that?

Thanks for the sage advice, buddy. I'll get right on that. Idiot.

"I did try," I say, "but she was with her friends. They swarm her, I swear." Henry scoffs. "Sounds like fish in a barrel."

I shake my head. Of course he doesn't understand the problem. He's never *had* this problem.

"I was going to see if she'd end up walking alone." I realize how creepy this is and quickly add, "To talk to her, obviously. As they were walking out, I heard her talking about work. She has a shift tonight."

"Where does she work?"

"McDonald's. She and her roommates all work there. I gu—"

Before I finish explaining how I learned this, the hood of the Chevelle slams shut and my roommate is in the driver's seat revving the engine, egging me on.

"Well, let's go. I'm hungry."

"I need Simba."

That's the first thing he says to me when I get in the car.

The engine is uproariously loud, so I think I heard him wrong. "What?"

"I need Simba. Well, I *want* two Simbas, but I need at least one."

"What?" I ask again. Sometimes he does this: starts talking and expects me to catch on.

While he pulls out another cig, he says it slowly, like I don't know who or what Simba is. "Siiiimmmmbbbaaa. You know, Mufasa's son. From *The Lion King*."

Shaking my head I ask, "What does a fictitious talking lion have to do with any of this?"

"I have Zazu, Timon, a couple Pumbas, Mufasa, Nala, Scar, and Rafiki. I have, like, three Rafikis. Would love to get another Nala, but it probably won't happen."

I've decided to stay silent.

Without further explanation, Henry reaches in the backseat and comes back with a plastic bag and hands it to me. I reach my hand inside and pull out three of at least twenty *Lion King*–themed Happy Meal toys. The plastic eyes of Scar, Mufasa, and Zazu stare in different directions.

"You've gotta be shitting me. You collect these things?"

He smiles with his cig between his teeth. "Bro, these things are going to be worth a fortune in ten years. Mark my words. I'm going to be RICH! So rich I can buy more Chevelles and Camaros and my own McD's and then I'll have access to every single toy I could ever want. Then that's more money. In the long run."

I don't know what to say to that because WHAT DO YOU SAY TO THAT?!

"Well," I say, "whatever you think is best."

He confidently nods and says, "So, what're you gonna say to your girlfriend when you see her?"

Did he just use the g-word? "She's not my girlfriend."

Ignoring me, he says, "What're you and your girlfriend going to do on your first date?"

I won't win so I just answer the stupid question. Which is actually a good question because I guess I never really thought about it.

Well, I guess I have. . . .

"I don't know, coffee or something."

Henry shakes his head. "McDonald's sells coffee."

Shit. That's a good point.

"Well," I say, "I did have one idea, but I'm not sure."

"Anything's better than coffee, college boy."

"I was going to ask her if I could borrow some books. Like, children's books. I don't have any, and I need some for next semester when I do field work with students. One day in class she said she'd been building her future classroom library. So, I figure she has to have some. We're also supposed to practice reading out loud before we go into classrooms and—" but I'm cut off.

"Ahhh, I see your game," Henry says. "You're trying to get a 'bedtime' story, aren't you?"

I'd punch him, but he'd punch me back twice as hard. So I

stick to calling him names relating to the swine that he is.

We pull into the parking lot and that's when I start to feel uncomfortable. What if she's actually in there? What am I going to say? The book thing? Stick to coffee? What if she says no? What if she laughs? What if she throws a McFlurry in my face?!

"You nervous?" Henry asks.

"No," I lie. He can tell.

"Just remember, when you ask her out the *worst* thing she can say is yes." He says this like he's some Greek philosopher bestowing invaluable wisdom unto peasants.

"What?"

"The worst thing she can say is yes to a date," he repeats. Then adds, "Think about it: if she says no, you're embarrassed and sad for a night, maybe two. But then you're back on the wagon right after that! But, if she says yes, you might have a good time on your date. Then there might be a second one. Then a third. And before you know it, you're wearing polo shirts, sporting loafers, going to brunch, and worst of all, what if she uses woman voodoo and you become . . . a Swifty! *Gross*." He genuinely looks concerned.

"You need to calm down. I'm sure there's enough blank space in your head to enjoy T-Swift's sweet nothings."

I pause, waiting to see if he's caught my puns.

"Her music sucks."

I ignore his comment. "But you're probably right. If she says no, I'll just shake it off. I don't want any bad blood."

I can't help myself.

✦

The smells are greasy, and the line is short, but I have plenty of time to survey the restaurant like the weirdo I am. By the time we order, get our food, and sit down, it's obvious I was nervous for no reason.

No McFlurries are thrown. She doesn't say no. She doesn't say yes. "She isn't here," I say.

Henry sips his Sprite, then his Coke. One for each of his Happy Meals. "She's not? Thank god."

I begin to ask how this is a good thing, but he's already reached into his cardboard boxes of happiness and pulls out the plastic toys, and unlike his meal, Henry is not happy.

"Another Rafiki and Scar! I swear, dude, this shit is rigged. They only give the Simbas to snot slingers. It's discrimination is what it is. Been thinking about suing."

I drink my Sprite in silence.

I'm not even halfway through my hamburger when Henry wads up his wrappers and breaks down his Happy Meal boxes. "Hurry up. Let's go."

"Where?"

"To find Simba and Swifty."

✦

Today is the day. The last day of class. Well, not every class. But the only one I really care about. The one with polka dots.

The sun is out, the sidewalk is mostly dry, and I didn't forget my sunglasses this morning.

Even better, no beer breath. But it came at a cost.

Upon our quest to find a fictitious, plastic lion, and my not-girlfriend, we had no luck at the second McDonald's location.

Or the third. Or the fourth.

Or the seventh.

Unfortunately, we are two small-town boys who were raised

by small-town, old Gen X-ers. Being polite isn't a behavior; it's a blood type. You *will* order something when you walk into a restaurant and eat everything you order.

THERE ARE STARVING CHILDREN WHO WOULD GIVE ANYTHING FOR YOUR PRIVILEGE! EAT YOUR FOOD!

Doesn't matter if it's McDonalds and you're ~~stalking~~ looking for someone. You will be polite.

So, because of that, for the next few hours, we ate the equivalent of five or six dinners, give or take. By the last couple stops, I was ordering a small fry and a cup for water. And, because of that, my stomach required me to be within view of the bathroom for the next twenty-four hours.

So much for fitness goals. Thank god Henry told me he was paying after the second stop. I tried to protest, but he's always been a better dancer.

But that's all in the past now. Because I'm actually five minutes early to class. Going to find a good seat. Perhaps even talk to her before class starts.

Alas. Turns out being five minutes early to a class full of education majors means you're six minutes late and almost everyone has their laptops out, Hydro Flasks in hand.

No big deal. It's all good. If anything good came from Tuesday's Ronald McDonald fiasco, it's something Henry said. It was in between a lot of stupid stuff, but even broken clocks are right twice a day.

"At the end of the day, if you want something that bad, you'll go get it," he said.

Granted, he said this a few minutes after he tried to bribe a fifteen-year-old cashier for a Simba toy, but you know, broken clocks.

So, here I sit, now almost done with class. Less than two minutes to go. And the worst thing happens.

Polka Dots packs up her things, gets up, and leaves. It doesn't seem like she's angry—more like she has to be somewhere soon. The professor is still yammering along, and Olivia (that's her name, by the way!) is almost halfway out the door.

I want to get up and go after her. But I can't. That would be too weird. Even too weird for me.

So, instead, I sit and wait and glance back and forth from the clock to my professor, wishing unspeakable evils upon her for not hurrying the fuck up and ending class. But, still, I sit quietly, because I'm an adult.

When the eternity ninety seconds is up, I'm the first one out the door, shoving the brass panel.

I turn left and the hallway is empty, but when I turn right, I see something even worse: Olivia is standing there, not even twenty yards away. But I can't go talk to her. Because she's talking to someone.

A guy.

And their body language looks . . . well, it's obvious.

I quickly turn left and try my best to walk away casually. I should have known better. Of course she has a boyfriend. Just look at her. How could I have been so utterly stupid to think someone like that wasn't already pursued? He's probably pre-med or pre-law. Or even worse. Finance.

I make it to the door, trying my hardest to find fresh air, already planning the lie I'm going to tell Henry. *Ah she wasn't in class today!* or *The professor asked her to talk after class and I had to leave.* He won't believe me, but he'll pretend to. After all, he's not just a roommate.

But I don't make it to the door. At least not right away. There's a tap on my shoulder. I turn around and it's her. Olivia. "Hi!"

God, her smile. It should be illegal.

I say the cleverest thing I can think of. "Oh, uhh, hey."

"I'm sorry to just run up on you like this!" She says it like it's an imposition and not the highlight of my collegiate career.

"Ha!" I say, "Well at least you don't have a knife. You're not trying to murder me are you?"

Oh my fucking god. Why am I allowed to talk? Knife? Murder? Where is the nearest hole I can crawl in?

Her straight face catches me off guard. "You're not someone worth murdering, are you?"

For a split second, I'm caught in fear. Did she think I was serious? I'm about to apologize for my stupid joke when I see the corner of her mouth begin to curl.

Again, I try to think of something clever, but thank the Speaking Gods, nothing comes.

Luckily, she adds, "I know I don't know you, well other than from class. But I wanted to ask you something."

My whole body goes warm, and for a second, I forget to expel the air from my lungs after letting it in. Is this it? Is SHE asking ME out? But what about her boyfriend? Maybe it wasn't her boyfriend. Probably just a friend.

"What's," spit gets caught in my lungs, so I have to clear my throat, which is awesome and not embarrassing at all. "What's up?"

"Well, I was at work the other night..."

Right away, my brain thinks of greasy sweat, and I hold my stomach as a Pavlovian response.

"... and I was talking to my roommate about our CKI fundraiser coming up."

"What's CKI?" I ask without thinking.

"It's a service club here at school. We do different projects to support our community, mostly people in need."

So, let's review. She's smarter than anyone I've ever met. Disney Princess type of beauty. And spends her free time making other people's lives better?

"Oh, that's cool! Could I join? I did community service in high school!"

Again. Why am I allowed to talk? That "community service" I did was forced by our principal and our parents for putting all of the dumbbells in the weight room in the shape of male genitalia. Well, *I* didn't do it. Henry did. I just took the pictures, got them printed, then sold them to people around school. They were tasteful, we thought. Principal Frasco didn't think so.

I'm not proud of it. I'm just explaining how I ended up serving pancakes at the Veteran's Breakfast my junior year of high school.

I said I was polite. Never said anything about smart.

"Oh!" she says caught off guard. "Sure! Absolutely! New members can join anytime. We meet every other Thursday night."

"Excellent," I say. I've decided this is the smartest thing I've said this entire conversation.

"We'll be so glad to have you!" she says. "But there was something else I wanted to ask you."

"A what?!" Henry's cig almost falls out of his mouth.

"I know. I know. I couldn't believe it either."

"Was she joking? You sure this is real?"

"Yeah. Well, no. I'm not sure which question you want me to answer. It's real. Here. Look at this."

I hand him the flyer Olivia gave me earlier.

The way he reads it, smoke wafting around him, he looks like one of those old-timey mechanics that's just been handed paperwork for a job. He reads the title out loud.

"'CKI Dating Auction!' Holy bear shit. This IS real."

He reads on for a few seconds before handing the flyer back, a black smudge where his thumb held the paper.

A stupid smile covers his face. "Soooo, like a piece of meat, she wants to auction you off to make money?"

"Shut up. It's for charity. All the money made goes toward helping those in need to get winter gear after New Year's. Hats, gloves, coats. All that. Like an after-Christmas Christmas."

"Sounds like a scam."

I roll my eyes. "How is this a scam?"

"A pretty girl—well, you claim she's pretty. For all I know, she's not even real. Anyway, a pretty girl, who isn't stuck up enough to have a job and is also the president of her charity club, wants you to help her raise money by auctioning you off to the highest bidder for a date?"

"More or less."

"Yeah. Scam for sure," he laughs.

I jut out my chin. "How do you figure?!"

"If she wanted to actually make money for this thing, you'd be the last person she'd ask. I mean, you own a mirror."

I let him enjoy his moment before saying, "Oh, yeah. One more thing. She asked if I knew anyone who'd want to be part of it. You know, anyone else who would be willing to help out and be in the auction. You know, any single friends."

I pause, letting him do the mental math.

"Oh, hell no. No!" He's so insistent he takes the cig out of his mouth. "No fucking way. Not uh. Nope. Never. This is your lake of bullshit and I'm not swimming through it, too."

"Oh, come on. It'll be fun."

"No! And besides, I already have plans for New Year's."

"What do you have to do?"

"Surgically remove my toenails with a butter knife."

"Dude."

"DUDE!"

"It's one night. Free food and beer at the auction. Plus, whoever 'buys' you pays for everything. And it's just a date. Ice cream or bowling. Something chill. And like I said, all the proceeds go toward helping people in need. People in our community. This is big stuff, dude. Last year they raised $7k in two hours!"

Henry puts his head out like this is new information. "Really?"

I smile. I knew he had a soft spot. "Yeah, man," I say. "Every single penny. Hats. Gloves. Jackets. Coats. Warm socks. For people who actually need it and—"

Henry waves his arms, so I stop.

"No," he says. "Not that. The part about the free beer and food. Really?"

The next couple weeks drag on. I passed my classes. Grades were fine. Nothing to brag about. Definitely not going to be asked to be a teacher's aid for Freshman English.

Christmas was tolerable. The same intrusive questions followed by the same partly comical, mostly evading answers. When Grandma Joyce asked if I'd met anyone special or when Grandpa Gary asked if I'd had a new fling, I just smiled and said, "I've had a lot of dates at the library. Good thing assignments don't make you buy them dinner!"

Everyone laughed and sipped their wine while I thought a little about the auction and a lot about polka dots.

But alas, New Year's Eve has finally arrived. The buzz of the New Year is more than just the couple of beers Henry and I had before we left for the auction. The feeling of something new, something fresh, was afoot. I'd started a new workout at the gym and was drinking (a little bit) less. I'd even started reading a new book, not even for school but for my own enjoyment. For a lack of many, many better words, I would say it was . . . refreshing. Yeah, undoubtedly refreshing.

Tonight was the night she was going to ask me out. I knew it. I could feel it. Why else would she have asked me to come to the auction? We'd never talked before, and that's the first thing she says to me? To raise money, sure! A woman like her could get any guy to do whatever she wanted. But she didn't ask just any guy. She asked ME. Someone she hardly knew. Why else would she have asked me?

I thought Henry would try to bow out at the last moment, but actually, by the time I'm ready, he's already on the front porch, inhaling and drinking his appetizer. He's wearing a T-shirt and jeans with a pair of Jordans. Not exactly impressive, but it works for him, which frustrates me because I ironed my best polo and wore a pair of slacks I haven't worn since high school. The waist is trying to strangle my stomach.

Henry scoffs and laughs as he says, "Jesus, took you that long just to look like you invite kids into your van. Let me guess, you have a puppy for me to pet and chocolate for me to try."

I hate that he's right.

We take the Chevelle because, in Henry's words, "I look too fucking good to be seen in your shitty Corolla."

We arrive at the college and make our way through the Student Center. The first thing I notice is how quiet the halls are. When school is in session, this place is a zoo with stressed-out students milling everywhere. Now it seems like a deserted Olympic Village. The few people that we do see are walking ahead of us, and since they're dressed up, I figure they're safe to follow. I might go to this school but that doesn't mean I know where everything is.

After what feels like a billion steps, we make it to the ballroom. Right away, my nose smells wings and my stomach tries to guide me. But my eyes scan for polka dots. It's a weird feeling, when your senses compete for dominance. But there's really no competition at all. Polka dots over fresh buffalo wings.

It's a square room about the size of a basketball court with rows of folded chairs, and at the front of the room is a big screen, and next to the screen is a microphone. I see a few of her friends setting up chairs, but Olivia is nowhere in sight. I decide she's elsewhere, getting things organized for the night, so I turn to Henry to tell him we should go snag some wings. But when I turn, he isn't there.

I do two full turns before I see my roommate. I shake my head and walk over to the small, makeshift bar in the corner of the room. As I walk up, he's dropping a tip in the jar and handing one of his two beers to someone I know. Lauren sat one chair down from Olivia in class, usually sipping on her Hydro Flask (Stanley's weren't popular yet) or chanting the class mantra of "I agree with Olivia."

But we aren't in class and Henry isn't Olivia. Lauren's eyes are fielding whatever bullshit he's dropping. The mechanic sips his beer while Lauren chugs his words. Christ.

"My man!" Henry raises his beer as I walk up. "I was just talking to . . ." He looks at Lauren and gives an embarrassed smile.

"Lauren," she says. Like it's a compliment he's already forgotten her name. "Yes! Lauren says she had a class with you! How studious," he says, winking.

This is so awkward, but I do my absolute best to make matters worse by sticking my hand out to shake hers like I'm meeting the god damn president.

Hesitantly, and clearly for the sake of impressing Henry, she puts her hand out. "Hi! Happy New Year's Eve!"

I just nod because I'm certain that speaking won't improve the situation. "Thanks for coming! Liv will be so happy!"

I smile, but I don't catch on that *Liv* means "Olivia," and by the time I do, Lauren is waving her hand, trying to get someone's attention.

"Liv! Liv!"

I turn and just about drop my beer. It's like she fell out of the Disney Tree and high-fived every princess on the way down. I have to consciously tell my jaw to pick itself up off the floor.

When Olivia—sorry, Liv—walks up, it's Henry who speaks first. But when he does, he speaks with a smile loud enough for all three of us to hear. And even worse, he looks at me when he says it.

"Stan, you liar! She doesn't look like a squirrel! And her feet aren't that much bigger than your average clown!" His accusatory tone is playful, but it doesn't matter.

I make a mental note to fill my pillowcase with rocks and beat him to a pulp when he goes to sleep tonight. I don't even care that Lauren will probably be right next to him when I do it.

I quickly look at Liv, who is definitely caught off guard. Lauren is smiling like she's not sure what else to do.

Oddly enough, Liv laughs. And I realize it's the first time I have a favorite sound.

Once she's gathered her hahas, Liv says, "What have you been saying about me?"

"I didn—!" I begin to protest, but she cuts me off.

"Sure!" she says playfully. "We'll have to talk about that later.

I need you two 'strong men' to come set up chairs behind the screen. My little squirrel arms aren't strong enough, and I might trip over my clown feet."

As we follow her, Henry and I exchange quick punches to the arms and elbows like a couple of kids following their mother in a grocery store. I'm swinging for revenge; he's swinging for laughs.

When we make it to the screen, my elbow and shoulder hurt and Henry's smile is almost to his ears. Liv directs us to the chairs and explains how she wants them set up. Before she leaves, Henry asks the ever-important question: "Do I have to put my beer down to do this?"

"No. A real man should be able to handle it."

The task should have taken five minutes, but it takes ten because we can't resist the urge to try and impale each other with the legs of the chairs as we "work."

Now my elbow, my shoulder, and my groin hurt. But I quickly forget my pain when I look around the screen and a sea of humans are sitting in the rows of what used to be empty seats.

"Holy shit! There's a ton of people here!"

Henry smiles and chugs the last of his beer. "Good! More lasses to bet on me!"

There's so much wrong with that statement I don't even know where to start. *Lasses? The fuck? Betting?* I shake my head and wonder how he isn't legally obligated to wear a helmet and a muzzle.

But my thoughts are cut short because CinderBeauty is at the podium.

"Hi everyone! Thanks for being here tonight! We're about to start! Could all of the participants please come to the screen if they haven't done so already! The auction will begin in a couple minutes."

Within a minute, there are nineteen of us: ten boys, nine girls.

All seated behind the screen. Henry is assigned to seat 12, and I got seat 19. Next to me is an empty chair, which means someone didn't show up.

When everyone is settled, one of Liv's friends is at the podium, and again, Liv has disappeared.

"Hi everyone! Welcome to the annual CKI Dating Auction! We have some very, *very* good-looking dates for you tonight!" The friend pauses to allow for applause. "Thank you so much for participating in this fundraiser. Our goal is to raise $8,000 for families in need of winter wear. That means beanies, stocking caps, gloves, sweaters, coats, really anything to help people stay warm during these bitter Colorado winters. Obviously, *toys* for kiddos are always appreciated! So, if you have any of those items to donate, please drop them off in the bin at the back. Please get some wings and a tasty beverage throughout the auction, as all proceeds will go toward our cause. Every dollar spent tonight will go toward families in need. As always, additional financial donations are never expected, but always appreciated. . . . Okay! Before we begin, our club president has a little treat for all of you. Liv, whenever you're ready!"

All of us in the chairs crane our necks to get a glimpse. Since I'm in seat 19, I have no chance at witnessing the big reveal. But it doesn't matter. Because I quickly learn that I have a second-favorite sound.

For the next minute, the opening song to the animated Disney classic *101 Dalmatians* serenades the entire room. The pitch of the clarinet is so good I'm sucked back to my childhood. I see Pongo prancing around the London flat to Roger's tune. But, of course, it's immediately ruined when my roommate leans over his seat and looks my way. Like an idiot, I lock eyes with him. Even though there are seven people between us, Henry shamelessly mouths, "Band geek!" Then smiles. Then pretends to play an invisible clarinet.

I decide that rocks aren't enough for the pillowcase and therefore add shards of glass to my fantasy.

I mouth the word *stop*, which he thinks is *hilarious*.

Rocks, shards of glass, and marbles. I make another mental note.

Liv is halfway through the song when her friend at the podium starts to talk over the music.

"Alright, my friends! It's time to find your Pongo or Purdita! We may not have one hundred and one, but we do have twenty lovely New Year's Eve dates for you! Let's find you the perfect Dalmatian!"

Obviously, the friend at the podium doesn't realize there's only nineteen of us, but whatever.

She pauses and smiles at Liv, who continues the soft melody of the song but at much softer volume. As the music plays, the friend turns back to the crowd and talks while Liv plays.

"Okay! Let's get started! Will our first Dalmatian please come to the stage? First, we have Kyle!"

At his cue, Seat-1-Kyle gets up and walks up next to the podium where the crowd can see him. There's a few whoops and hollers, but nothing crazy. "We are going to start the bidding at fifteen dollars!"

"Twenty!" one girl says.

"Twenty-five!" says another.

Eventually, after a minute or so, Dalmatian Kyle is sold for forty-seven dollars.

As soon as Kyle disappears, a terrifying thought enters my brain. What if Liv doesn't bid on me? Is she going to play during the entire show? If she does then . . . What if *no one* bids on me?

By the time the eleventh Dalmatian is auctioned off, I am in full freak-out mode. I contemplate getting up to leave but decide that getting caught sneaking off would be worse than not receiving a bid.

I look down and realize Henry is up next. Happy as a clam, he looks like he's about to meet Santa. When he gets up to the stage—no, it's as soon as he crosses the threshold of the screen and is exposed to the crowd—it's like Mount Vesuvius erupts and he's the goddamn geographical plates that caused it. The hot lava of cheers and screams from the crowd are deafening.

And, being the humble humanitarian my roommate is, Henry feeds into the love of the crowd and begins barking and gyrating the same way a horny dog would. He looks like a fucking idiot. Mostly because he is.

Fifteen minutes, almost *two* fist fights, and NINE HUNDRED AND EIGHTY-THREE DOLLARS later, he's sold.

Great. He goes for almost a thousand dollars, and I probably won't go at all.

After Henry leaves the stage, it's like the wind is knocked out of the room. Two more guys are auctioned off: one for sixty-three, another for ninety-seven.

After the second guy leaves the stage, the friend at the podium says, "Give it up for Liv!" Everyone claps and cheers. Not nearly as loud as they did for my dipshit roommate, which is a wild injustice, but whatever.

Another clarinetist takes over and I crane my neck again, but Liv is nowhere in sight. At first, I figure she's taking a break, maybe getting a drink at the bar or running to the restroom.

But then it hits me.

No she isn't. We've only been here an hour, probably less. She's in the crowd. She's gonna bid on someone. *Someone* she probably *specifically* invited. I abruptly sit up in my chair with my chest out.

Tonight is going to turn out awesome after all!

The next three Dalmatians bids move quickly and go for less than fifty dollars each. I'm bobbing my head to the melody played by the new clarinetist and life is good. I start wondering where Liv and I will go. Bowling? Ice cream? Axe throwing? Disney World? I don't give a shit. All four, hopefully.

I'm looking at Dalmatian 18 as they head up to the stage with a big smile when I feel a nudge on my side. I look over, and it's the worst and best thing ever.

It turns out, all of the participants *did* show up. In seat 20 sits the equivalent of two Disney princesses.

"So a squirrel, huh?" Liv says as she nudges my side again with that damn smile.

I'm so caught off guard I try to protest, but finding words is like trying to catch air with my hand.

She giggles. "I'm just kidding. I like this polo. Purple is definitely your color."

"Henry said I look like a pedophile."

Did I just say the word *pedophile* at a charity event? I don't know why I say the things I do. Being an idiot just comes naturally.

"Well that would make him friends with a pedophile then. And I think that says more about him than it does about you. Besides, he's a dumbass."

If I had a ring at that moment, I swear to God I'd have a bruised knee. Instead, I give a small laugh. "Yeah."

"You'll probably go for a million."

"What?" I ask.

But she doesn't get to answer. Because right then Dalmatian 19 is called up to the stage.

Of course she has a boyfriend. What was I thinking? How could I not see that? Liv wasn't flirting with me; she was being nice. Even more, she was trying to raise money for her club.

I wanted to be mad, wanted to feel used. But what had she done wrong, really?

Helped me get a date while also helping people in need? That was her crime.

Yeah, being mad at anyone but myself would be stupid. Still, I wondered what she was doing tonight. Where had her boyfriend, the one who bid on her at the auction, taken her? A movie? Dinner? A Mediterranean cruise?

All of these ideas, realistic and not, haunted my brain the days following the auction—the first days of a brand-new year that were *supposed* to bring a brand-new me, remember?—but even more so tonight as my ice cream becomes soup. My date, kind as she is, can tell I am here physically, but only so.

"Are you okay?" she asks.

I begin to answer, but as I do, the bell over the door rings.

And Liv walks in with her boyfriend.

Immediately, I pretend to be wildly interested in my date. "Yes, sorry. I was just wondering what we should do after this. Bowling? Movie?"

She smiles, and I feel horrible. But I can't let Liv think I'm having a bad time. And maybe if I pretend to have a good time, eventually I will.

And maybe I won't think about polka dots, or Disney princesses.

Especially when I'm with someone who paid $147 for my time.

But all that goes to shit within two seconds.

"Stan!" Liv shouts as she approaches our table. I could listen to her say my name over and over again forever.

I look up and do my absolute best to act pleasantly surprised. My customer service voice isn't so bad.

"Liv! What are you doing here?"

"Aaron and I just got done with dinner and wanted to get some dessert!"

She thumbs back at her boyfriend standing in line. He's staring at his phone smiling. He doesn't look up even though he can easily hear us. The place isn't that big.

"Nice!" I say. *Yikes*.

"Thanks so much for coming to the auction," Liv says to my date.

My date smiles and nods. "Of course. Such a good cause! I loved this year's theme, by the way. I hadn't thought about that movie in so long."

"I liked it, too. One of my favorites as a kid. Gotta love Pongo and Purdita's story," I add. Because I'm a nerd and can't help myself.

Liv smiles at me with her eyes, and she's about to agree, I think, but my date keeps going:

"And you found such good-looking Dalmatians!" She nods to me, and I blush, feeling worse.

I'm a piece of shit for being on this date and thinking of Liv and then wanting to impress Liv, and I know it.

"Liv!" the boyfriend in line calls.

I think we're done with this interaction, but then my date says, "How much money did you make? Did you hit your goal?"

"Oh, you must have missed the announcement that night," Liv says. She sighs. "We made less than half our goal. We only reached a little over $2,500."

I have to admit that's kind of disappointing.

"That's too bad! Sorry I couldn't give more!" my date adds.

"Liv, hurry up!" the boyfriend calls again.

Liv puts her hand up, signaling for him to hold on, then turns back to my date.

"Oh, no way! Anything and everything helps. Really, it does!" The way she says it, it's not customer service. It's real.

"And besides," she adds, "we actually ended up making our goal after all. After the auction, the president of the college called me about a bag that had been dropped off in her office."

The impatient boyfriend all but yells from fifteen feet away: "Liv! Let's go! Holding up this line!"

And before she turns to go order, she tells us inside the bag was an envelope. In the envelope was a bunch of cash and a few coins. In all, totaling $6,969.69.

And below the envelope were countless unopened McDonald's toys.

Just as she finally turns to leave, Liv says, "After I'd counted the money and gone through the toys, I reeked of cigarettes. But hey, we made our goal!"

And that's where the story ends. There is no dramatic blow up. There is no Aurora and Prince Phillip. No Ella and Charming. No Simba and Nala. No Disney ending to this story. Well, not like those stories, at least.

Because a month later, I'm finishing my second day in the classroom as a partial student teacher. It's the best. I'm confident this is what I want to do forever.

Sharing the art of story with kids is truly the best thing. There's no doubt. I even started writing my own book. It's about a good friend of mine and losing him too early in life. It's a heavy tale, and I'm a shitty writer, right now at least. But it'll get better. There's always another chance.

It's a new year. A new start.

I'm not dating anyone, and I don't need to. I want to focus on teaching and my writing. I don't have time fo—

My phone buzzes.

It's an email, so I swipe. I see the name, and I read the name. But instead of words, all I really see are polka dots.

Dark purple and pink.

I drop my eyes to the contents of the message. It's one sentence, a question.

Pongo,
You don't have any children's books I could borrow, do you?
Purdita

About the Author

Mitchell S. Elrick lives near the mountains in Colorado with his wife and pets. When he isn't teaching sixth-grade language arts or coaching basketball, he's tip-tapping at his computer, usually cursing that he can't find the right words. (Much like he did writing this blurb.) If he's not teaching, coaching, or computer-cursing, he's usually losing to his wife at *Mario Kart*.

You can find Mitchell on:
Instagram @mitchellselrick.author

Contributors' Library

Please also look for these titles, which were authored by, published by, or feature the authors in this anthology.

Bad Idea Lane
A Novel
Krista Renee

Library Lovebirds
Short Stories
Katie Fitzgerald

The Bennetts Bloom
Flash Fiction Stories
Katie Fitzgerald

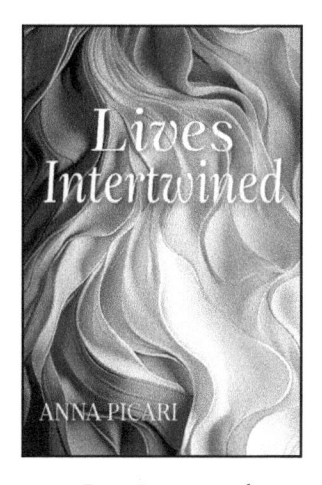

Lives Intertwined
A Novel
Anna Picari

Done
Charlestone Harbor, Book 1
Desi Stowe

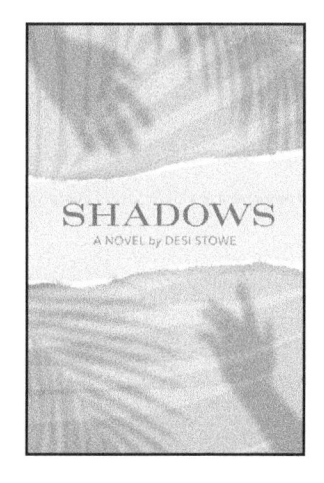

Shadows
Charlestone Harbor, Book 2
Desi Stowe

About the Editor

Nicole Frail has been editing fiction and nonfiction books for adults and children for fifteen years. Between 2012 and 2024, she worked as an acquisitions and project editor for a traditional publisher based in New York City while simultaneously working with independent/self-publishing authors via her small business, Nicole Frail Edits.

In mid-2024, she switched gears and decided to take her "side gig" full time, expanding the services offered through Nicole Frail Edits, LLC. Shortly after, she formed her own small press, Nicole Frail Books, LLC, to publish anthologies born out of short story contests as well as ebooks and other projects still to come.

Nicole lives just outside Scranton, Pennsylvania, with her husband, three little boys, and two Tuxedo cats.

You can find Nicole Frail on:
Instagram @nicolefrailedits & @nicolefrailbooks
Facebook @nicolefrailedits & @nicolefrailbooks

And visit her websites at www.nicolefrailedits.com
& www.nicolefrailbooks.com

Mini Acknowledgments

I ran out of room and didn't want to ask for a new template, etc. so quick thank-yous to: Kerri Odell for cover and interior elements; Elizabeth Cunningham for first reads; Amy Applegate for final reads; Sydney Ahrberg and Shawn Carey, my interns from Wilkes U.; Plunge Into Books Tours; the NYE authors who patiently waited for their turn while I used the Winter anthology as a test subject and then who worked impressively fast alongside me to get this out! And, of course, and always, Matthew, Cooper, Travis, and Eli. ♥x4